P9-EJU-292

THE PHANTOM TOWER

ALSO BY KEIR GRAFF

The Matchstick Castle

The Other Felix

THE PHANTOM TOWER

KEIR GRAFF

G. P. PUTNAM'S SONS

For the kids in Room 322, who read it first

G. P. PUTNAM'S SONS
an imprint of Penguin Random House LLC
375 Hudson Street
New York, NY 10014

Library of Congress Cataloging-in-Publication Data
Names: Graff, Keir, 1969– author.
Title: The Phantom Tower / Keir Graff.
Description: First edition. | New York, NY : G. P. Putnam's Sons, [2018]
Summary: "When the missing button for their new apartment building's thirteenth floor suddenly
appears, identical twins Mal and Colm are pulled into an eerie adventure in an parallel dimension"—
Provided by publisher.
Identifiers: LCCN 2017053084 | ISBN 9781524739522 (hardcover) |
ISBN 9781524739539 (ebook)
Subjects: | CYAC: Brothers—Fiction. | Twins—Fiction. | Adventure and adventurers—Fiction. | Single-
parent families—Fiction. | Apartment houses—Fiction. | Blessing and cursing—Fiction. | Supernatural. |
BISAC: JUVENILE FICTION / Family / Siblings. | JUVENILE FICTION / Lifestyles / City & Town Life.
Classification: LCC PZ7.G751575 Ph 2018 | DDC [Fic]—dc23
LC record available at https://lccn.loc.gov/2017053084

Printed in the United States of America.
ISBN 9781524739522

1 3 5 7 9 10 8 6 4 2

Design by Jaclyn Reyes.
Text set in Goudy Old Style MT.

Brunhild Tower Apartments

4300 Marine Drive CHICAGO, Ill.

1930's finest new residential building faces
the **LINCOLN PARK GOLF COURSE** *and* **MONTROSE YACHT HARBOR**.
It is mere steps from **CLARENDON BATHING BEACH**.

Live in Georgian grandeur and enjoy the gilded elegance you deserve
with **DOORMEN**! **ELEVATOR ATTENDANTS**! **CAR PORTERS**!
at your beck and call.

(Accommodations for live-in maids are available.)

These exclusive homes for discerning Chicagoans
are brought to you by the **KRAYFISH CO**.

LEASING AGENT ON-SITE—VISIT TODAY OR CALL 555-9973

CHAPTER ONE

CHICAGO

THE FIRST TIME I saw Brunhild Towers was the day we moved in. Even though it wasn't that long ago, I saw a lot of things differently back then. I thought old people were boring. I thought learning history was a good way to fall asleep. I thought dying was simple.

You probably noticed I said *Towers*, not *Tower*.

Pay attention and I'll explain everything.

• • •

Mom had been driving all day with my brother, Mal, and me in the back seat. The air conditioner in our old van barely worked, and the August heat was making us sweaty, tired, and crabby. My right arm was red and sore from where Mal had been punching it, and Mal's left arm looked even worse—I was better at using my knuckles.

Mom's voice was fried from telling us to knock it off. Every few miles she tried again.

"Malcolm. Stop arguing."

"Malcolm! Stop hitting!"

"MALCOLM! If you make me pull over and stop this car, you'll lose all your screen time for a week!"

She was talking to both of us, actually. You see, Mal's full name is Malachy, and my name is Colm. Whenever we're in trouble, Mom drops the *and* between our names and we become Malcolm.

The screen-time threat was the only one that worked. Mal's favorite thing is building stuff in *Minecraft*, and mine is wrecking stuff in video games—Mal says I'm just a griefer, but I prefer to think of myself as a demolition expert—so the idea of being grounded from screens after we finally got out of the car was a nightmare.

Still, I just don't think there's any way you can put twin brothers in the back of a minivan for the 926-mile drive from Dallas to Chicago without both of them needing to throw a few punches.

After two days on the road, we were positively sick of each other. We were sick of the way the upholstery rubbed against our sweaty legs, and we were even sick of fast food. All my favorite foods come from drive-through windows, but if I had to unwrap one more burger or breakfast sandwich, I was going to projectile vomit all over our minivan, and we would need to call in a hazmat team to make it habitable again.

The van was so full of stuff, it was almost impossible to move. The space behind us was crammed with boxes. Our feet were resting on duffel bags full of clothes, so we couldn't even straighten our legs, and we had to hit each other over Eric the cat, whose carrier was on the seat between us. The front passenger seat had a lamp, a computer, and our TV in it, which was strapped into the seat belt to protect it from disaster.

If you're wondering why our dad wasn't in that seat, well, it's because he's dead. He was in a car accident two years ago, when Mal and I were ten. Dad was the one who named the cat Eric, but I still don't know why. I've asked him, but he just laughs.

I know what you're thinking: I'm crazy, because you can't talk to dead people. But you're wrong. You *can* talk to them. You're only crazy if you expect them to answer you. I talk to Dad all the time, just to hear his voice in my head. Who cares if I'm making up all the stuff he says? Even so, sometimes I'm afraid he'll stop answering.

Sometimes I'm afraid I'll forget what his voice sounded like.

Moving was Mom's idea. She never even asked what we thought about it. One day, she just told us it was time for a fresh start. She said she had gotten a new job in Chicago and we were leaving in the middle of August. I didn't want to go. I wanted things to stay the same, but it seemed like ever since the policemen came to our door the day Dad didn't come home from work, our old life had been falling apart piece by piece.

Mal didn't like to talk about moving, or Dad, and I hated making Mom cry, so Dad was pretty much the only one I had to talk to.

• • •

Chicago traffic made Dallas traffic look minor league. It took us an hour and a half to get from the big green *Welcome to Chicago* sign above the highway to our new apartment.

By then, the sun was going down, and I was so hungry that I might even have been able to eat a cheeseburger without spraying it all over the back seat.

Finally, we turned right, and Mom swore and hit the brakes. She swears sometimes, but Mal and I act like we don't hear it. If we swear, that's a different story. She can hear it a block away.

"There it is: Brunhild Tower," she said. "I missed it!"

Then, instead of going around the block like a normal person, Mom backed right down the street, ignoring all the honking horns, while Mal and I scrunched down in our seats and tried to hide. Eric moaned like he was embarrassed, too.

When Mom pulled into the driveway, I couldn't see much—all the stuff crammed into the van blocked the view. But I could tell it was old and fancy: Through the windshield, I glimpsed gray stone, big windows, and some flowers and plants, if you care about that kind of thing.

Mom stopped in front of four tall gray pillars and climbed out of the car.

"Wait here and don't try anything," she said. "I'll just check in with the doorman."

When we heard the word *doorman*, Mal and I exchanged a look. In our old house, you had to jiggle the key in the lock forever before it worked. And in the apartment we moved into after Dad died, we had to enter a key code to get into the building. But we had never lived in a building with a doorman.

"Maybe Mom's new job pays a lot better than her old one," said Mal.

"Who knows?" I said. "She wouldn't even tell us if she won the lottery."

Mom never talked about money. I knew things were tighter now that Dad was gone, but it wasn't like we were rich or anything before that. Still, Mom always tried to act like everything was just great. Like she didn't mind working a part-time job in the evenings and like having a giant old box of a TV was somehow better than having a flat screen like everyone else. Like it was somehow better for Mal and me not to have cell phones when the fact was we just couldn't afford them.

Mal usually went along with her and pretended, but it drove me crazy. It's embarrassing not to have a cell phone or a flat-screen TV. We were lucky our computer wasn't made out of wood.

Mom came out of the building with a man wearing a black-and-gray uniform. The man pointed at something behind us, and Mom got back in the car.

"Who's that?" I asked.

"That's the doorman, dummy," said Mal, taking advantage of my being distracted to hit my arm right on the bruised spot.

I had my fist raised to retaliate when Mom stopped me with a look. So I sent him a telepathic message instead: *I'll get you later.*

"His name is Virgilio," said Mom. "He said there's parking behind us. We can't bring our boxes through the front door—we have to go to the loading dock. But I think it's too late to unload, don't you?"

"Yes," we said at the same time, not wanting anything to get between us and dinner.

We had to drive back onto the street to get to the parking lot. Fortunately, this time, there were only a couple of honks. The way people in Chicago laid on their horns, you'd think they drove horn-powered cars.

Inside the lot, Mom parked in the numbered space Virgilio had given her. Then we got out of the van and stretched. Mom started pulling things out of the back while Mal and I had a quick kickboxing battle that I totally won.

"Malcolm, *enough!*" snapped Mom, holding out things for us to carry.

We took our duffel bags, backpacks, the cat carrier, and the litter box and headed across the lot to the main building.

Brunhild Tower loomed over us, huge and dark. Above the gray stone on the first few floors of the L-shaped building, black iron fire escapes zigzagged up the redbrick walls that faced the parking lot. It was so big,

I felt like it would swallow us up. Suddenly, a stupid hope occurred to me: What if we couldn't find our apartment? Since we weren't unloading the van, we could just drive back to Dallas.

It was still hot as an oven outside. The heat coming off the blacktop practically melted the bottoms of my sneakers. I'm no expert on big cities, but it did seem weird that there was room for such a big parking lot when there were so many tall buildings crowded around.

Mom stood there for a moment, staring up at the building with that look she gets that makes me think she's going to start crying.

"Your dad would have loved this place," she said. "He always liked older buildings. He said they were built to last."

I tried sending Mal a telepathic message: *Quick, change the subject.*

"Why is it called Brunhild Tower?" he asked. Studying his face, I couldn't tell if he'd gotten my message. He probably just asked because he's always going out of his way to learn things he'll never need to know.

"I have no idea," said Mom, snapping out of it. "But it sounds like something out of an old folktale, doesn't it? *Brunhild.*"

"Sounds like a witch's name," I muttered as we started walking toward the building.

None of us had any idea how close Mom and I were to being right.

CHAPTER TWO

BRUNHILD TOWER

VIRGILIO THE DOORMAN seemed like a pretty nice guy. He was short and wide, with jet-black hair, round eyes, a flat nose, and the widest smile I had ever seen.

"Welcome to Brunhild Tower!" he said, grinning and shaking my hand as I came into the little entry room behind Mom.

Then, when Mal appeared behind me, he exclaimed, "Wow—there are two of you!"

People always say a lot of dumb stuff when they meet identical twins, like, "I must be seeing double!" or "When they made you, I guess they *didn't* break the mold!" Fortunately, Virgilio moved on before Mal and I had to decide which one of us would pretend to laugh at the joke.

"So, how old are you guys?" he asked as he shook Mal's hand, too.

"Twelve," I told him.

"So that's . . . what grade?"

"We're going into seventh," said Mal.

"Do you guys like football? Are you going to watch the Chicago Bears?"

"Mal's a mathlete," I told Virgilio. "And he's into *Minecraft*."

"What's your sport? Baseball? Basketball? Hockey?"

I didn't really know how to answer. Dad was a big rugby fan and used to tell us all about it—and we used to play soccer, but since he died, Mom had been too busy to sign us up for teams.

"He likes messing with the things I build in *Minecraft*," said Mal.

Still looking confused, Virgilio asked, "Which one of you is older?"

Now, *that* is an annoying question people always ask twins. I mean, just because I'm one and a half minutes younger, suddenly *I'm* the little brother? It's a meaningless distinction, and the last thing Mal needs is encouragement.

"I am," said Mal, grinning and poking himself with a thumb.

"By, like, ninety seconds," I added, elbowing him in the ribs.

"And how do people tell you apart?" asked Virgilio.

Mom smiled. "They can't. That's the problem."

"Not even you?"

"It depends," said Mom. "If I've been with them

for a while, I can always tell. But if one of them walks into the room and I forget what they've been wearing, sometimes it even takes me a minute."

And if we swapped clothes, I thought, *like we sometimes used to do before Dad died, she had no clue at all.*

Mal looked at me and smiled, like he was remembering the same thing.

"Okay, final question," said Virgilio. "Can you read each other's minds?"

"No," said Mal, at the exact same moment I said, "Yes."

"You guys need to get your story straight," chuckled Virgilio.

Oh, we will, I thought at both of them—but nobody heard me. Lots of twins have reported unusual psychic connections, from being able to read each other's minds and finish each other's sentences to just knowing how the other one is feeling. I knew Mal and I could have this power, too, if he stopped being so uptight about it and let me read his mind. But he kept it zipped up like a winter coat.

The building manager was gone for the day, and Mom had to sign something before Virgilio could give us the keys to our new apartment. Once that was done, he told us which elevator to use and then opened the inner lobby door that let us into the building itself.

It was nice having someone open the door for us, but it was also kind of strange how we had to wait for him to do it. It made me feel special but also a little bit rude.

When I whispered that to Mom, she agreed. "But it's also his job," she said. "So we should let him do it and respect the way he earns his living."

The little entryway where we'd been talking was nice enough, but the actual lobby was super fancy. There was an old fireplace right in front of us, with two chairs and a small table, and tall halls going off to the left and right. Glass chandeliers hung from the ceiling, and there were paintings of lakes, rivers, and prairies on the walls.

My first thought was that it looked like a hotel out of some old movie. A really old-fashioned hotel. I mean, where else do you see furniture in the hallway?

My second thought was, *There's more than one elevator?*

"Virgilio said to turn left and then it would be on the right," said Mom.

We turned left and looked right, down a long hall with evening light coming in through high windows on our left. We walked to the end of the hall and found an elevator. A small metal plate next to the elevator said *01-02*.

"That's not right," said Mom, shaking her head. "Our apartment number is 1404. We're in the wrong tier."

"Tier? What's that?" asked Mal.

Like I said, Mal has to know *everything*.

"There are three elevators in this building, and each elevator serves two apartments on each floor. Each stack of apartments is a tier. We must have walked past ours."

We retraced our steps and found another elevator

where we'd first turned right. The place was so elegant that even the elevators blended into the scenery.

The metal plate beside the doors read *03-04*.

"That's it," said Mom. "We walked right past it."

I pushed the button and looked up to see a semicircle of brass numbers just above the doors. After a moment, an arrow started moving counterclockwise through the numbers as the elevator started to come down.

"I know what you're thinking," I told Mal.

"You do not," he said.

I did know what he was thinking at that moment, though, even if he wasn't transmitting his thoughts: He was missing our old place, where he knew where everything was and how it all worked. With its tiers and hidden elevators, Brunhild Tower was completely different from our old apartment building. But I knew he was also starting to feel a little bit curious about our new home.

Just like I was.

"I know what *I'm* thinking: I can't believe we got this apartment, especially on such short notice," said Mom. "All the other places were smaller and more expensive. It was so nice of my new boss to give me a recommendation."

The elevator doors opened. It sounded like there was an old-fashioned bell trying to ring, but something was stuffed inside. Instead of *DING* it went *TINK*.

"How many floors are in this building, Mom?" I asked as the doors closed behind us.

"Check out the buttons, stupid," said Mal, nodding at the panel next to the doors.

I punched him in the arm and then looked. The highest button was labeled *17*.

"Seventeen floors," I said. "What's our apartment number again?"

"1404," said Mom.

"We are going to have a rockstar view," said Mal.

I looked at the buttons again and pushed *14*. Then I noticed something weird: The button below ours was *12*.

The elevator doors closed, and we started going up.

"There's no 13," I told Mal and Mom.

"People used to be superstitious about the number 13," said Mom. "They thought it was unlucky."

"That's called triskaidekaphobia," said Mal with a smug smile on his face.

I thought about punching him just for knowing that but decided to save it for something more annoying. Because it *was* kind of an interesting word.

"They would leave out the number thirteen whenever they could," continued Mom. "Most old buildings don't have a thirteenth floor."

"Well, they do—" I started to say.

"But they're numbered fourteen," said Mal.

I glared at him. When Mal finished my sentences, it wasn't because he was reading my mind. It was because he couldn't help interrupting me.

"So when you think about it, we're on the thirteenth floor," Mal explained, just to make sure we all knew he had figured it out.

"I guess you're right, Mal," said Mom. "It's a good thing we're not superstitious."

Speak for yourself, I thought. I'm not afraid of unlucky numbers, but I still think there are a lot of things we don't know, if you know what I mean.

The elevator stopped, and the doors opened with that same *TINK*. We stepped out into a short hall with doors on the right and left. There was a lamp on a table, and four framed pictures on the wall showed what looked like Chicago in the olden days.

"I don't know if this is a room or a hallway," I said.

"It's called an elevator lobby," said Mom. "It's like a waiting area for these two apartments."

Right then, Eric meowed really loud.

"Better hurry—I think he has to use the litter box," said Mal.

Mom unlocked the top lock, then the bottom lock, and pushed the heavy front door open. She turned on the lights, and we squeezed past her and ran into the apartment. I put down the cat carrier and took a look around.

CHAPTER THREE

APARTMENT 1404

THE FIRST THING we noticed was that the place was *huge*. In our last apartment, you could practically see the whole thing as soon as you walked in. Here, all I could see were halls and doors.

"Slow down, guys!" laughed Mom, opening the door of the carrier so Eric could come out.

But we were already running around, turning on all the lights, going down the hallway to the right (where there were two bedrooms and two bathrooms) and the hallways to the left (where we found the kitchen, an empty room, another bathroom, and a hallway to the dining room) before finally working our way back around to the giant living room. The view stopped us in our tracks.

It was a corner room, and out the windows on one wall, we could see a harbor, a park, and the dark water of Lake Michigan with the setting sun making the clouds glow pink. Out of the windows on another wall, we could see white headlights and red taillights as cars sped along a highway Mom said was called Lake Shore Drive. In the distance, a crowd of skyscrapers shot straight up, their windows sparkling with light.

The view was so distracting, it took me a while to notice something else about our new apartment: It was full of other people's furniture. There were couches and chairs in the living room, a table and chairs in the dining room, lamps in the corners, and even paintings on the wall.

"Are you sure this is the right apartment?" I asked. "It's full of someone else's stuff."

"This apartment comes furnished," said Mom. "And even if we hadn't sold our old furniture at the yard sale, we barely would have had enough to fill one room of this place—it's so big."

Unlike the furniture in the lobby downstairs, the couches and chairs in the apartment didn't look like they came from a hotel. They looked like they came from someone's house. The cushions were so flat you could practically imagine people sitting in them, and there were a couple of stains that made you wonder if they were sloppy eaters.

It wasn't nice and new. It was weird and old.

"It smells funny," I said.

"Nothing a little fresh air won't fix," said Mom cheerfully.

"Let's open the windows!" said Mal, of course going along with her.

"Though it would be nice if this place had air-conditioning," added Mom.

We went around opening windows and letting in hot, humid air—along with some big spiders that had made giant webs on the outside of the windows. We flung them back outside with a newspaper, and then we washed our hands in the bathrooms, which looked like they were a hundred years old.

When I turned on the faucet to wash my hands, what came out was a reddish-brown liquid. It looked like blood.

"MOM!" I yelled.

When she poked her head around the corner, I pointed at the sink.

"I think this place is haunted," I said.

"Oh, that's just rust in the pipes," said Mom. "Let it run a minute; it'll be fine. Old buildings are full of surprises."

Finally, Mom ordered some pizza. While we were waiting, Mal and I went downstairs to fetch my pillow and Eric's cat food from the van. As we walked through the lobby, I was kind of looking forward to seeing Virgilio again, but he wasn't there. There was a different doorman sitting at the desk, skinny and old with wisps of gray, curly hair.

When we came into the vestibule, I expected him to say hi or something, but he just stared at us with dark, glittering eyes as he slowly stood up and moved toward the door.

“We’re new—we just moved into 1404,” said Mal, trying to be friendly.

The doorman didn’t say anything. I noticed he had a small name badge pinned to his shirt that read *Dante*.

“We’re just going out to the parking lot for a second,” I said. “We’ll be right back.”

Dante still didn’t answer. Going about as fast as a one-hundred-year-old man wading through maple syrup, he opened the door for us. Then he stood there watching silently while we walked to the parking lot.

“Well, that was bizarre,” I said as soon as I knew he wouldn’t be able to hear us.

“You don’t have to tell him where we’re going,” said Mal.

“I just wanted to make sure he’d let us back into the building,” I said.

Mal didn’t say anything, which was his way of telling me I had a good point.

The odd thing about Brunhild Tower was that, even though we had keys to our own apartment, we didn’t have a key to the front door.

I got my pillow and Mal got the cat food, and then we double-checked to make sure the van was locked. The night was noisy, with a soccer game across the street, a booming subwoofer in one of the cars lined up at the intersection, and a police siren screaming down Lake Shore Drive.

We couldn't see much, though, because the parking lot was surrounded by a hedge and a tall metal fence. Fireflies floated near the bushes, rising and falling and winking out like sparks over a campfire.

The fireflies reminded me of home.

"Well, Colm," Mal began, "I don't think we're in Texas anymore."

"That's exactly what I was thinking!" I told him. "Twin telepathy! Now let me read your mind."

Mal rolled his eyes. "Go for it."

I closed my eyes and concentrated really hard, imagining my brain waves were invisible tentacles that reached out and wormed their way into his skull, slithering into the wrinkles in his brain until his thoughts were revealed. I saw Mal standing on the roof of Brunhild Tower, turning in a slow circle as he checked out the view.

"You wish we could find a way up to the roof!" I said.

"Nope. I'm thinking there's no such thing as telepathy."

I punched his arm and then ran for the building before he could punch me back. What an absolute jerk.

Dante was waiting just inside the door. He opened the outer door for me and then held it until Mal caught up. Then, while we waited in front of the desk, he walked in slow motion to the inner door. It was like watching a sloth try to run a hundred-meter dash. Finally, he reached the inner door, unlocked it, and held it open for us without saying a word.

“Thank you,” we mumbled.

While we waited for the elevator, Mal whispered, “I can see why they put him on night duty.”

◆ ◆ ◆

It took me a long time to fall asleep that night. Mal and I were sharing the big bedroom at the other end of the hall from Mom’s. Even though I was tired, and even though we were high up on the fourteenth floor, I could still hear horns, sirens, and roaring motorcycles, in addition to jet planes. The city at night was so bright, the windows glowed, even with the shades pulled down.

“Mal? Isn’t this place weird?” I whispered, pushing down my musty sheet.

“A little,” he said sleepily.

“I feel like I’m in Grandma and Grandpa McShane’s house, only it’s not as nice.”

“At least we don’t have to worry about breaking Grandma’s precious figurines,” said Mal.

Still feeling sweaty, I kicked my sheet all the way off. “I wish we were still in Dallas. Don’t you?”

“Well, we’re not, and we’re not going to be, so you may as well get used to it. Just try to be nice to Mom, okay? It’s not easy for her.”

“It’s not easy for us, either,” I told him.

Mal didn’t say anything, but that wasn’t unusual. He doesn’t like talking about things that really matter.

A little while later, I whispered, “Mal? I can’t sleep.”

Again, he didn't answer. I guess he didn't have the same problem. I reached into my pillowcase for the two most important things I own: Dad's watch and phone. Mom knows about the watch because she gave it to me after the funeral at the same time she gave Dad's pocketknife to Mal. It's an old-fashioned watch that winds up, and I wind it every night so I can hear it ticking while I fall asleep.

She doesn't know about the phone. I found it in a kitchen drawer filled with batteries, earbuds, and charging cords, and I just took it. It's a flip phone and was still sealed in a baggie that said *evidence*. I guess the police had taken it from Dad's car after the accident and given it back to Mom. I kept it because it made me feel closer to Dad, like I could just call him if I really, really needed him. I had never charged it, though. I think, in a way, I was afraid that if I called him, it might work—I'd really be talking to him instead of imagining what he said.

I know how stupid that sounds.

I wound the watch and put it in my pillow, its soft *tick-tick-tick* like a metronome, or a heartbeat. Then I wrapped my hand around the phone.

Dad? What do you think about this place? I asked. *I know Mom said you'd like the building, but what about the apartment? Isn't it creepy?*

I didn't get an answer—maybe because I wasn't sure what he would have said.

Mom can go for days or even weeks without talking about Dad, like it hurts too much to think about him, but other times, out of nowhere, she starts sharing random memories. Like how he was such a hard worker, or how he had an amazing singing voice. Sometimes she sings his favorite songs, which makes me feel embarrassed for some reason, even though she's not a bad singer.

I think she's trying to make sure we don't forget him. Some of her stories are great, like the funny one about how he talked his way into his first job when he got to America from Ireland: He told the foreman he was a skilled forklift operator because he was really good at eating. But in other ones, he seems like a character out of a book, strong and wise and funny. He was all of those things, but sometimes he lost his temper, too, just like Mom does nowadays.

I have my own memories of Dad, but they're fading. Sometimes when I try to picture him doing something, it's like waking up from a dream where I tell myself I'm going to remember it this time for sure, but it's already running away from me like water on the beach.

Mal may be scientific and rational, but I'd rather be a little superstitious. I don't believe in vampires and werewolves and stuff like that, but it might be nice if ghosts existed. That way, Dad could always be with me—haunting me in a good way—even if I forgot him.

Squishing my eyes together so tight it actually hurt, I thought as hard as I could: *Dad, are you still there?*

I held my breath until it felt like my lungs were about to burst before I heard his voice over the soft ticking of the watch.

I'm still here, Colm.

His voice was so strong, I almost fell out of bed. It was like he was lying next to me with his head on the pillow.

Mal was right: Mom wasn't going to let us go back to Dallas. But even though Brunhild Tower was strange and old and wrong, at least Dad was coming in loud and clear.

I didn't want to be there, but in a weird way, I hoped we'd stay forever.

CHAPTER FOUR

THE BUTTON VANISHES

WE SPENT THE NEXT DAY, Sunday, unpacking, cleaning, and exploring the neighborhood. Mom started her new job on Monday, and we were going to begin school two weeks later. Summer was almost over, even if it didn't feel like it.

We found lots of leftovers in our new apartment. A couple of our dresser drawers still had clothes in them, like some shirts and pants that might have fit Mal and me but were so old they looked like they came from a yard sale. There were socks and underwear, too, but I didn't even want to touch those, so I made Mom take them all out.

There was other stuff, too—not a lot, but just enough to make us wonder if the apartment had ever really been cleaned out between renters. Mom found old baking spices and a cooking pan in the kitchen, and Mal found a junk drawer with some batteries, pens, and takeout menus from before the internet was invented. I found a bag of golf clubs in the hall closet and a dusty electric razor in the bathroom.

Mal and I each had our own closet, and on the shelf at the top of mine was a cardboard box with some ancient-looking school notebooks that apparently belonged to a kid named Teddy. There were also some baby shoes, a silver rattle, and a yellowing envelope with blond hair tied in a blue ribbon inside.

"These things don't even look like they all belonged to the same person," said Mom. "It's like every family who ever moved out left something behind."

"If we move out, I'll leave all my homework for the next kid," I said.

Mal rolled his eyes. "You'll scare them away. Everyone will think this place is haunted."

"If you both keep using that word, *I'll* start to believe it," Mom told us. "Now help me move this stuff to the room off the kitchen until I have time to deal with it."

That room, which had its own little bathroom, was the only one that was completely empty. Mom said it probably used to be a bedroom for a maid who lived with the family she worked for. I quickly noticed that if you stood in its closet, you could hear voices and water running in pipes—sounds that disappeared the moment you stepped out.

When I showed Mal, he wasn't impressed.

"It's just noise from other apartments, stupid," he said.

"I know that, genius," I said.

I didn't tell him what I really thought—that the

murmuring voices sounded like ghosts. In our old apartment, the only sound I ever heard was the neighbor's TV. The little bedroom creeped me out. I was glad when Mom said it would be her home office and a guest room if anyone came to visit.

Between the kitchen and the dining room was a hall with a long counter and cabinets on either side that Mom called a butler's pantry.

"A maid's room and a butler's pantry," she said. "This place was built for richer people than us!"

Just before lunch, Mom took us on a long walk around the neighborhood so we would know where everything was.

Across Lake Shore Drive, to the east, there was a giant park with a hill, soccer fields, a golf course, and a boat harbor, and a little farther away, a long, sandy beach.

Across Montrose Avenue, to the north, there was another park with a soccer field, tennis courts, softball fields, and a field house. To the south, on Hutchinson Street, there were old mansions that looked like they cost millions of dollars.

"I still can't figure out why the rent is so low in such a nice neighborhood," said Mom, staring through a tall iron fence at a stone mansion that looked like a castle. "I just can't!"

"Maybe our building has rats," I suggested.

Mal slugged my arm. "It doesn't have rats," he said.

"Maybe it's cockroaches," I said, slugging him back.

"Maybe we're just lucky," said Mom, but she didn't seem convinced.

We started walking again. Across the street, a girl with frizzy black hair, bright orange sneakers, and a backpack over her shoulders started walking, too. I noticed she had been behind us for a few blocks, checking out the houses and stopping when we stopped. But before I could say something to Mal, she disappeared around a corner.

The last place we visited was our new school, a concrete structure with dark windows that looked like it was made out of giant building blocks. From the sidewalk, I couldn't even figure out where the front door was.

"That's our school?" I said. "It looks like a prison."

"It's not a prison, Colm," said Mom with a sigh.

"It probably feels that way to him," said Mal, Mr. Understanding.

Everybody thinks identical twins are, well, identical. But even though Mal and I look the same, we're different in lots of ways. And the biggest way we're different is that Mal loves school. And why wouldn't he? He's on honor roll every year, and the teachers are always wearing out their thesauruses looking for new ways to tell him his test scores are "superlative" and his reports are "keenly insightful." When I get compliments, it's for stuff like writing in a straight line.

Most maddening of all, Mal acts like the reason I'm behind is because he's a minute and a half older than me. And I always *have* been behind: When we were learning to read, Mal was reading picture books out loud while I was still memorizing the alphabet. When we were learning times tables, Mal knew them up to twelve while I was still stuck on fours and fives. And now that we're doing fractions and graphs and variables and stuff like that, Mal is in heaven and I'm in the other place.

Mom keeps saying that I have lots of talents, too, but I'm still waiting to find out what they are. One of my biggest talents is putting up with my brother, but I'm not perfect at it or anything.

When we went behind the school to see the playing fields, the girl in the orange sneakers was there again, wearing headphones and sitting on a playground swing. It didn't seem like she was paying any attention to us, but it was hard to tell behind her big sunglasses.

On our way home, I saw her one more time, looking at the books inside a Little Free Library. I poked Mal and pointed.

"She's been following us," I whispered.

"She can't be following us; we're walking toward her," observed the Human Computer.

"She was behind us before—I think she knows where we're going."

"But *why* would she be following us? Whoever she

is, I'm sure she has better things to do than follow you around, Colm."

Mal shook his head and rolled his eyes while he said it, which was a big mistake: He didn't see my Knuckles of Doom coming.

"Ow! Quit it, Colm," he said, rubbing his arm.

"Moving along, Malcolm," said Mom, turning the corner.

When we got back to Brunhild Tower, Virgilio wasn't there to open the outer door for us. He was inside the vestibule, talking to an old man who barred the way with the canes he held in both hands. Old maybe, but big: He had a hunched back and looked like gravity was catching up with him, but he was still the tallest one in the room, with a burly chest, a huge head sprouting thick, white hair, and a long, white beard.

"Good afternoon, Mrs. McShane," said Virgilio. "This is Professor Parker. Professor Parker, meet Mrs. McShane and her sons, Colm and Mal."

I liked that Virgilio said my name first. That almost never happens.

"So you're Professor Parker!" said Mom, squeezing between us to shake hands with the old man—he switched the cane in his right to his left so he could do it. "What are you doing here? Do you live in this building as well?"

"Oh no," said the Professor. "I . . . just thought I'd stop by to see how you're settling in. So these are the twins I've heard so much about."

He squinted at Mal and me like he was trying to spot the difference and then shook our hands, too. His hands were massive, warm, and damp—it felt like reaching inside a roast chicken.

Mom must have finally realized our confusion. "Mal and Colm, Professor Parker will be my new boss at the University of Chicago. He was the one who helped us find this great building."

The Professor smiled proudly. "I hope you're finding everything to your liking."

"The apartment is wonderful," gushed Mom.

Of course she left out the smelly old furniture, so I chimed in. "The people who used to live here left a lot of stuff—"

"Colm!" Mom interrupted with a nervous laugh. "Professor Parker doesn't care about *that*. I'll just contact the management company so we can return the previous tenants' belongings."

The Professor raised an eyebrow at Virgilio.

"That apartment has been empty for quite some time, ma'am," said Virgilio. "I think it's safe to say the former occupants won't be coming back for their things."

"I'm surprised such a nice place would stay empty for long, especially in this location," said Mom.

"We have quite a few empty apartments. Some people just don't like to live in older buildings like this."

"On the other hand," added the Professor, stroking

his beard like it was a pet, "some people find it impossible to leave. I hope you'll be happy here."

"Oh, I know we will," said Mom.

Then the Professor did what no one should ever do and asked, "Did you have a good trip?"

What followed was one of those grown-up conversations that make you feel like time has stopped. The only interesting thing about it was that it gave me a chance to get a better look at the Professor's canes. One had a worn brass eagle's head for a handle, and on the other one, which had a knobbed head, I could see a small, carved face peeking out from between his fingers. Both of them looked a hundred years old.

Meanwhile, Mom and the Professor entered full getting-to-know-you mode while Mal and I slumped deeper and deeper into the bench across from the doorman's desk. The Professor was better at asking questions than answering them, though. In fact, by the time Mom finally said we'd better be going, he seemed to have learned our whole life story without saying anything about himself.

And even though he was talking to her, he kept looking over at us. His mouth was smiling and his voice was warm, but his eyes seemed to be measuring us somehow. I'll be honest: He gave me the creeps.

"I shouldn't keep you any longer when I know you have so much to do," said the Professor finally, turning and clomping toward the front door, planting a cane before he moved each foot. "A pleasure meeting you, too, boys!"

"See you bright and early tomorrow!" said Mom, making it sound like she was going to work in a cotton-candy factory.

"I'll see you, but not bright and early," chuckled the Professor. "I should warn you that I keep irregular hours."

That makes perfect sense, I thought as we rode up in the elevator. Everything about the Professor seemed irregular.

I glanced at the control panel and saw the *14* button wink out as we arrived at our floor. But I was taking off my shoes in the apartment before I realized what else I had seen.

A button for *13*.

I ran back out into the elevator lobby, called the elevator, and then stepped inside to make sure I hadn't imagined it. But the button was gone.

CHAPTER FIVE

THE WRONG ELEVATOR

THE NEXT DAY, Mom woke us up early. She had already showered and done her hair and was dressed up for her first day on the job. I knew what was coming next: the Lecture.

"Now, I'm expecting you boys to behave responsibly because I don't want to come home from work and get a bad report from our new neighbors," she began.

"Do we even have any neighbors?" asked Mal sleepily. "I sure haven't seen any. Not in the lobby, not in the elevator . . ."

"We have to have some neighbors," I said. "I can hear them when I'm in that creepy closet."

"More importantly, *you'll* know whether your behavior has been appropriate," continued Mom. "I am trusting you not to spend the whole day in front of a screen, to eat some healthy food, and to stay out of trouble. If you go outside, I want you to stay on this block."

"We will," we promised in unison.

As soon as we heard the door close behind her, we

jumped out of bed, poured bowls of cereal, and turned on the TV. Mom used to threaten that if she got one of those "bad reports," she'd hire a nanny to watch us, but Mal and I had long since figured out that the reason we were on our own was that we couldn't afford one to begin with.

A couple of hours later, Mal left so he could work on Malandia, the world he was building in *Minecraft*. I had been banned from Malandia for flooding the basement of his castle, building volcanoes in his amusement park, and releasing thousands of cats onto his chicken farm, so I plugged our gaming system into the TV and played *Kart Krashers* until I got hungry for lunch.

After another bowl of cereal, I wandered over to watch Mal at the computer. It took me a minute to figure out what he was working on.

"That's our apartment!" I said.

"No duh," said Mal.

In response, I tried to give him a dead arm. I don't think it worked, but it was enough knowing I made him mess up what he was working on. Instead of hitting me back, he just swore and fixed it. If you don't have a brother or sister who's always hitting you, a dead arm is what happens when they hit you right on the nerve with their knuckles and your whole arm goes numb.

"Why?" I asked.

"Boredom. I'm kind of stuck, though."

"What do you mean?"

"Well, there are six apartments on each floor. But I don't know what any of the others look like. For all I know, they're all completely different."

"You're doing the whole floor?"

"The whole *building*," said Mal. "Now go away so I can work."

"Why can't I watch?"

"Because your breath stinks."

I checked—he was right. I filled my lungs, leaned over, and exhaled right under his nose.

"I don't want to watch, anyway," I said, walking off while he gagged and tried to fan it away. "Especially if you're too stupid to figure out how to do the rest of it."

I headed for the front door.

"Where are you going?" he called after me.

I answered by grabbing the house keys. He caught up with me by the time I reached the elevator lobby.

"If you want to see what the building is like, look around," I told Mal.

"Don't be a moron, Colm. You can't just knock on people's doors and ask to go in."

"You heard Virgilio: A lot of these apartments are empty," I said, looking at the door across from ours. It had an old lion's-head knocker and the brass number *1403*.

"They're still not going to leave the doors unlocked."

"How do you know?"

I was acting braver than I felt, but it was too late to

stop. I put my head up against the door and listened. I heard some building sounds, like the elevator rattling up and some water gurgling down, but I didn't hear anything inside the apartment. I grabbed the handle.

"Don't do it," said Mal, in a tone that sounded a lot more like *Do it! Do it! Do it!*

The handle turned—but the door was locked.

"Epic fail," said Mal.

I didn't say anything. I just went back to our apartment, into the kitchen, and out again through the back door. There was another elevator lobby, not nearly as nice as the main one, for the freight elevator.

I looked at 1403's back door. No trash or recycling waiting to go out—and no paper waiting to be taken in.

I turned the knob. The door unlatched.

Inch by inch, I pushed it open. Behind it was an empty kitchen. Completely empty—and covered in a thin layer of dust.

"Epic success," I said.

Mal's eyes were as round as Ping-Pong balls. He looked nervous, but he followed me in, anyway. It was obvious that no one lived there, but I walked quietly just to be safe. Even from the kitchen, I could tell the layout was totally different, starting with the fact that there was only one way out of the kitchen.

Mal ran back to our apartment for a pen and a pad of paper while I tiptoed farther, almost holding my breath, still half expecting some big dude to walk around the corner and bellow, "HEY! WHAT ARE YOU DOING IN MY APARTMENT?!?"

But it really was empty. It was smaller than ours, with two bedrooms, two bathrooms, and a big long room for a living room and dining room that looked out on both sides of the building. It was disorienting to be right next door and have a totally different view.

I looked in some drawers and closets, but this apartment seemed truly, totally empty.

Mal was following behind, sketching the layout.

"Have you got everything?" I asked after he'd been through every room.

"Uh-huh," he said, nodding.

But he didn't follow me out. I looked back and saw him standing there, tapping the pencil's eraser against his lower lip.

"Do you think the other empty apartments are unlocked, too?" he asked.

This was not the Mal I knew. I was tempted to respond with another question: *Who are you, and what have you done with my brother?* Instead, I said, "You never know until you try."

"Where should we go next?" he asked eagerly, already getting a taste for crime.

"Well, if the apartments are the same on every floor, then we know what the 03 and 04 apartments look like . . ."

"So the logical thing would be to visit the 01-02 tier and the 05-06 tier," Mal concluded.

"Four more floor plans to go," I said.

We closed the door of 1403 and, since we were standing right by the freight elevator, pressed the button. The main elevator was nice, with wood on the walls and ceiling, but this one was all metal and felt like a meat locker. Plus, you had to push the door open yourself, and it must have weighed two hundred pounds.

We went down to the first floor and out into the lobby, sneaking past Virgilio at the front desk. Mal and I didn't have to read each other's minds to agree we shouldn't let anyone know we were trying to get into empty apartments.

We went down the south hall to the 01-02 elevator.

"Any floor, right?" I said, looking at the buttons.

"Why not the top one?" said Mal.

I couldn't think of a reason, so I pushed the button and the elevator started going slowly up, moving from side to side like it wanted to break out of the elevator shaft.

On the seventeenth floor, we looked at both doors before Mal shrugged and went to try the handle of 1701, which didn't have a nameplate.

"Maybe you should knock first," I whispered as he put his hand on the doorknob.

No sooner had he touched the handle than the door flew open and an old lady stood there scowling at us. She was dressed like she was going to a funeral in a black dress, a black beaded purse, and a hat with feathers that probably came from a crow she murdered herself.

Mal yelped, his hand suspended in the air where the doorknob had been.

"Und vair do you think you are goink?" she asked.

From her accent, I guessed she was Russian or something like that—and she looked a hundred years old.

"We took the wrong elevator by mistake," I blurted, impressed with myself because it was a decent excuse.

The old lady looked at me. Then she looked at Mal. Her skin was pale and wrinkled, like a piece of paper that had been folded a million times.

"You are new in thees building," she finally said.

I assumed that was supposed to be another question.

"We moved in on Saturday," said Mal.

Inside her apartment, an old grandfather clock gonged once, long and low.

Hearing it, she stepped aside and said, "You vill come een." She sounded like someone who was used to having her orders obeyed.

Mal and I looked at each other. I frantically sent him a telepathic message: *Don't do it! It's a trap!*

Of course, he didn't get the message. For a moment, I thought the new, adventurous Mal would turn around and run, but the old Mal was used to obeying orders. He did as she said and walked inside.

Which meant I had to follow, too—what was I going to do, leave him there?

CHAPTER SIX

THE PRINCESS

MAL AND I sat in the old lady's living room, listening nervously while she banged around in the kitchen. "Ve vill haff tea," she had announced, pointing us to the couch without even bothering to ask if we like tea, which we don't. And who drinks tea on a hot summer day? The windows were closed, and it was so warm we were already starting to sweat.

The room looked like a library in a greenhouse. There were books everywhere there weren't plants, and plants everywhere there weren't books. And in front of the books on the bookshelves were pictures, maps, stacks of coins, little figurines, snow globes, and other knickknacks.

I put my hand on a fluffy black pillow, which jumped up and hissed at me. The pillow was actually a long-haired cat that looked like it probably weighed twenty pounds and was one hundred in cat years.

I yanked my hand back as the cat licked itself, climbed onto my lap, and sat down.

"We have to get out of here," I told Mal.

He had a panicked look in his eyes, too, but he shook his head. "We can't leave."

"Why not?"

"What if she calls Mom and tells her we were trying to get into her apartment?"

"She might call Mom anyway."

"She probably just wants to lecture us for snooping around. If we listen to the lecture, maybe she'll let us go without telling on us."

"*You* listen to the lecture," I said, starting to stand up.

But as soon as I lifted myself off the couch, the cat growled and dug its claws into my legs, forcing me to sit back down.

I really was trapped.

Cups rattled in the kitchen, and then there was a clank that sounded like a kettle on a stove. When I looked over at Mal, he had his notebook out and was drawing the front door, the entryway, and the living room.

"I know what you're thinking," I said.

"It's obvious what I'm thinking, because the notebook and pencil are what you call *clues*," he said.

"If you would just *try*, we could have communicated all of that without saying anything out loud," I said with a sigh.

The old lady came back in and put a tray down on the coffee table. Or maybe it was a tea table. Could one table do both? I never know these things. She poured three cups of tea, put the cups on saucers, and placed a little cookie on each saucer.

Then she took her teacup and sat back in a red chair so tall it looked like a throne.

"I am Princess Veronica Margareta of Syldavia," she said. "Vot are your names?"

"I'm Mal, and he's Colm," said Mal.

"Und vot ees your *family* name?" asked the Princess.

"Our last name is McShane," said Mal.

"Are you really a princess?" I asked, reaching for a cookie. The huge cat flexed its claws, so I moved gingerly. My legs were so warm it felt like I had a pile of hot laundry in my lap.

"Yes," she said, looking at me sharply. "I am a real princess. Though my family lost its land und our castle a long time ago."

Mal and I didn't know what to say to that one, so we bit into our cookies. I tried to chew as quietly as I could, but the cookie was dry and it sounded like someone jumping up and down on a cardboard box.

"Your hand vas on my doorknob," she said, ignoring her tea and cookies, her large, watery eyes like searchlights. "You ver not lost."

Mal shook his head. He never could hold up under interrogation.

"You ver lookink for something," she continued. "But vot? Und who sent you?"

I swallowed. Now I was so thirsty I was actually considering drinking tea. "Nobody sent us, ma'am."

She frowned at the *ma'am*.

I tried again: "Mrs. Princess?"

"My full title ees Princess Veronica Margareta von Andelblat of the House of Hupburg. But eef you vish to be brief, a simple 'Princess' vill do. 'Mrs.' ees so common."

"He's telling the truth, Princess," said Mal. "We just wanted to see more of the building, that's all."

"You seem very intent on seeink thees particular part of the building," insisted the Princess. "For vot reason?"

"Well, Mal is working on a map—" I started to say, but she dropped her teacup and was up out of her seat before I could finish. She snatched the pad of paper out of Mal's hands and stared at it.

"You are spies! SPIES!" she said, her voice surprisingly loud for an old lady.

Suddenly, another cat—this one a big calico—jumped up on the tea table and started lapping milk from the little pitcher. The Princess didn't even notice.

"No, we're not!" I said. "We just moved into the building and we're curious about it and Mal was modeling it on *Minecraft* and we wanted to know what all the apartments looked like. We just picked this floor at random!"

She turned to me, her eyes as blue as the Arctic Ocean.

"Und een vich apartment do you live?"

"1404," I said.

"I see." She sat down again, picked up her teacup, and gave the big calico cat a shove, which it totally ignored.

"*Down*, Aslan," she said, but the cat kept drinking milk. "Do you see vot I haff to put up vith?"

I had missed them in the clutter, but now I suddenly realized there were cats all over the room: curled up on footstools, lying under chairs, and perched on window-sills. There was even one very small black cat sitting in a bookcase and looking out at me from between two old leather-bound books.

"Can I have my notebook back?" asked Mal.

"Yes, of course," said the Princess. "How rude of me."

Then, calmly, she tore off the top page—the one with the drawing of her apartment—and crumpled it up. She threw it over her shoulder, and a cat darted after it, batting it across the hardwood floor all the way into the other room.

Behind us, a tall grandfather clock went *BONG*.

"Von thirty," said the Princess as she returned Mal's notebook.

This was definitely the weirdest tea party I'd ever been to. Granted, it was the only one I'd ever been to, but the Princess wasn't acting like anyone else I'd ever met.

Then, as if things couldn't get any weirder, she suddenly started acting completely normal. Every time we tried to leave, she'd ask us another question: about Mom, where we were going to go to school, why we had come to Chicago, what Dad had been like and how he died, and who we had met so far.

We told her we hadn't met anyone except Virgilio, Dante, and Professor Parker—she flinched when I said his name.

"Und vot did Professor Parker tell you about thees buildink?" she asked.

"Nothing, really," I answered. "I mean, he said some people liked it so much they never want to leave, but it seems so empty, there can't be very many people like that."

I tasted my tea, but it was bitter and gross. I might have tried some milk in it if the big calico cat hadn't drunk it all.

"So there ees no reason you moved to Brunhild Tower een particular," said the Princess.

"Well, sure. Mom's new boss recommended it," said Mal.

"Und who ees your mother's new . . . boss?" the Princess asked, saying the word *boss* like it was low-class.

"Professor Parker," I said.

She froze. "Und he told you nothink else about Brunhild Tower."

"Just that it was affordable, I guess."

"Und he did not send you to my floor."

So she was getting weird again.

"No, ma'am," I said.

"He means 'Princess,'" Mal added.

How many times did we have to tell her—and why was she so obsessed with the Professor?

The Princess paused for a moment, looking like she was going to say one thing before deciding on something else. "Und how are you findink Brunhild Tower? Do you like your apartment?"

"The building is pretty cool, I guess, but the apartment had other people's stuff in it. Do you know who used to live there?"

"People come, they go, they go, they come," she said with a sigh. "Not all of them pick up after themselves. More tea?"

Our cups were still full. We shook our heads. The clock went *BONG BONG*.

"Just as vell. Two o'clock. All ees now safe. Time for you to go."

I couldn't wait to leave, but the cat on my lap wasn't going to let me. I had to put my fingers under its paws and then stand up suddenly to make it jump off.

At the door, the Princess suddenly got all stern again.

"Mal and Colm McShane," she said. "You must not come at lunchtime again. I don't eat lunch. Een fact, you should stay at home during this hour. Eet ees far healthier. But I do enjoy visitors—eef you vish to see me, simply ask Dante, und only Dante, to call up first. Und above all, do not go vanderink."

With that final warning, she shut the door. Neither of us said anything until the elevator came, like we were afraid she'd hear us if we did.

"Well, that was bizarre," said Mal after the doors closed and the ancient elevator car started its slow shimmy downward.

"Did she say 'All is safe'?" I asked. "What does that mean? And why Dante? Why not Virgilio?"

"And why is she so freaked out about the Professor?"

When the elevator doors opened, the girl in the orange sneakers was standing right in front of us. She didn't look surprised at all.

She folded her arms like she had all the time in the world.

"So you met the Princess," she said.

CHAPTER SEVEN

TAMIKA

"**HOW DID YOU** know that?" asked Mal.

"It's kind of obvious," the girl said. "According to the elevator indicator, you just came straight down from seventeen without making any stops. And there's only one resident on the seventeenth floor of this tier."

"Why are you following us?" I demanded.

She stepped back so we could come out of the elevator but still stood in our way. "Why would I be following you? You moved into my building. I can't help it if I keep seeing you around—in fact, it's kind of annoying. Maybe you're following me!"

This was escalating faster than I expected. "We had no idea you lived here," I said. "If we're following you, we would have figured that out already, believe me!"

"Well, now you know."

We all stared at one another for a moment. She had smooth brown skin and big sparkly eyes. Even though she was scowling, it looked like she might burst out laughing any second.

"Do you know the Princess?" Mal asked sheepishly.

"Everyone knows the Princess," said the girl. "She's lived here forever. Did she invite you in for tea? I hope you guys like cats."

"We have a cat," I said. "But I hate tea."

"What's your cat's name?" she asked.

"Eric."

"Huh. That's a pretty peculiar name for a pet."

I agreed with her, and I almost said so, except then I would have had to explain how Eric got his name and I didn't want to talk about Dad.

I shrugged, and the girl did, too. Slowly, she reached out a long index finger, like she was going to poke me in the stomach. Then she reached past me and pushed the button to open the elevator doors again.

She got in. "I'm Tamika, by the way," she said as the doors started to close.

"We're Malcolm," said Mal, just before the doors slid shut.

"Geez, Mal. Why did you tell her that? That's what Mom calls us!"

Mal groaned and hit himself on the forehead. "I don't know! It just slipped out."

I thought about not hitting him, because he'd already hit himself, but then decided he deserved it. Now Tamika thought we were called Malcolm and, if we saw her again, we'd have to explain it, so I lined up my knuckles and hit him as hard as I could on the side of his arm. Then I sprinted down the hallway to the 03-04 elevator.

Mal didn't chase me, though. He just walked back, rubbing his arm and shaking his head.

"I know what you're thinking," I told him. "That girl is strange."

"It still doesn't mean you have telepathy," said Mal.

• • •

Mal spent the rest of the afternoon working on *Minecraft* Brunhild Tower, adding the floor plan for 1403 and everything he'd been able to remember about 1701, the Princess's apartment. Then he did a little work on the outside, trying to get the landscaping and parking lot just right. I was tired of wrecking cars in *Kart Krashers*, so I made a fort for Eric in our bedroom out of blankets and moving boxes. He didn't bother exploring it—he just walked inside, lay down, and started purring. He was lucky he didn't have to share his space with a dozen other cats like in the Princess's apartment.

When Mom got home, she changed out of her work clothes and went straight to the kitchen to start dinner. At first I wanted to avoid her so I didn't have to say anything when she wanted to know about our day, but then I decided that the more I avoided her the more curious she would be—so I breezed into the kitchen and asked, "What's for dinner?"

That's when I noticed she was just standing at the counter, holding an open jar of pasta sauce, her shoulders shaking as she cried silently.

"Spaghetti," she said without turning around, wiping her cheeks with the backs of her hands. She was trying to make her voice cheerful, but it sounded strange, like she was gasping for air. "It'll be ready soon."

"Okay, thanks!" I said, already in the other room.

I hated it when she cried, and I felt bad pretending not to notice. Mom had gradually been getting less moody since Dad's death, but she still had what she called her "ups and downs." I was probably supposed to give her a hug or something, but for some reason, when I saw her heaving shoulders, I just wanted to get as far away as possible. Maybe I was afraid I would start bawling, too. And there was no use bringing it up with Mal, because he refused to talk about it.

She seemed normal enough when she called us for dinner a little while later. She had made spaghetti, garlic bread, and a salad we had to eat if we wanted seconds on garlic bread. Mal and I had agreed in advance that the best way to avoid telling her about our day was to ask about hers, but as soon as Mal started, I wished I had warned him about the crying.

"So, how was your day, Mom?" asked Mal.

"It was fine, thank you," she said, cutting her noodles with a knife. Mal and I are both twirlers.

He kept going. "Do you like your new job?"

She looked at the food on her fork. "Well . . . your dad always said you shouldn't judge anything on the first day."

"Is Professor Parker a nice boss?" I asked, right before I stuffed a big ball of spaghetti in my mouth.

Mom put her fork back on her plate. "I didn't even see him today! I was getting trained by a woman named Vonetta, and she wasn't the most friendly woman in the world. But I shouldn't be too hard on her. She could have just been having a bad day."

"Well," said Mal with a big, cheesy grin. "By definition, only one person can be the most friendly woman in the world—and that's already you, Mom."

He was going to blow it. If you have something to hide, the last thing you want to do is overcompliment Mom. It's like it flips her suspicion switch or something.

"That's sweet of you to say, Mal," said Mom, frowning and finally lifting some food into her mouth.

"How far away is the University of Chicago?" I said quickly, trying to distract her. "What does your office look like and how do you get there?"

As Mom turned to look at me, I realized that I had blown it. Asking more than one question at once is a dead giveaway.

All business now, she chewed, swallowed, and asked, "What happened here today?"

Mal looked at me. I sent him a telepathic message: *Lie! Lie! Lie! Or else we're doomed!*

He nodded, like my message had gotten through, and then went ahead and told Mom how we sneaked into the apartment next door and spent a whole hour in Princess Veronica's apartment.

Mom frowned while she listened. Her eyebrows got so scrunched up, I wasn't sure they'd ever get straightened out.

When Mal finished, he smiled, and I could tell he expected to get off easy for honesty.

"Malcolm, I am EXTREMELY disappointed," she said angrily. "Honestly, I'm not sure why I trusted you two to stay out of trouble! Sneaking into apartments and talking to strangers? If I can't count on you to make good decisions while I'm gone, I don't know what I'll do, but I'll do something."

We looked at our laps and nodded along. *Way to go, Mal.*

"I'll hire a nanny, or I'll take you to work with me. That poor old woman—you could have given her a heart attack!"

"Trust me, Mom," said Mal. "There's no way that lady's having a heart attack. She practically gave *us* one."

"And she's not poor; she's a princess!" I added.

"Don't get smart with me," snapped Mom. "Where did she say she was from?"

"Oh, Syldavia," I told her, grateful to change the

subject. "It's next to Rumoria. She talks like Dracula. She told us her family had a castle, but they lost it."

Mom stared at me, like she was deciding whether to chew me out for making up something so ridiculous.

Then she sighed and picked up her fork. "Well, I hope I get the chance to meet her soon so we can be properly introduced and I can apologize in person. But you two are not to bother her again. Do you understand?"

"Yes, Mom," we said, feeling lucky she hadn't said anything about taking our screen time away.

◆ ◆ ◆

That night, Mal fell asleep right away like he always does. I wanted to know what Dad thought about Princess Veronica, so I wound his watch, stuck it in my pillow, and held his phone while I thought about how he'd answer. I knew he liked old people and was patient with them—at least, that's what Mom always said—so after a while, I heard him say, *She's a crazy old gal, but she seems perfectly harmless.*

Was that what Dad would have said—and was that what he sounded like? It had been so long since I'd heard him in person, I was starting to forget. He had an Irish accent—what Mom called a brogue—but the voice in my head sounded like the cartoon leprechaun they used to sell cereal.

My hand was sweaty, so I pushed the phone inside

the pillowcase and kicked off the sheets. The ceiling fan churned the hot, humid air while traffic surged down Lake Shore Drive like waves breaking on the beach.

Grandma McShane in Ireland always said Dad was in a better place and watching over us, but why didn't he find some way to let me know? Was it like Mal and telepathy? Was Dad saying things to me I just couldn't hear?

It's never a good idea to start thinking about stuff like that when you're trying to sleep, but I couldn't help it. Mal was snoring faintly. I turned my pillow over to the cool side and tried to think about something else, like being an explorer who discovered the world's biggest pizza.

It didn't work. Even when I imagined climbing up a hot, golden crust as tall as a house, I pictured Dad looking down at me from the top.

Mom never said anything good about where Dad ended up. She believed in science, and science said dead people were just dead and nothing else. A dead person can't think or feel; they just decompose.

Fortunately, Dad had been cremated, so I didn't have to picture his body decaying in the ground. But in a way that was worse because it was like he'd just disappeared. Mom had given the ashes to Grandma and Grandpa McShane, who dumped them in some river in Ireland, so now they were probably swirling around in the Atlantic Ocean.

When I started imagining what it was like to be dead with only science to explain it, I got this cold, empty feeling in my stomach. The only thing that made me feel better was thinking about people having kids, and *their* kids having kids—like, Dad was dead, but I was alive, and someday I would have kids, and then they would keep me alive even after I died.

But that couldn't go on forever because scientists say someday the sun will die, and then there will be just cold, empty space where our solar system used to be. If we even last that long before climate change or nuclear war wipes everyone out. The thought of space going on and on forever without human beings really freaked me out.

If Mal was awake, he would have said, *Relax, dummy. Five million years from now, we will have figured out how to colonize other planets with interstellar travel, and there are earth-like planets all over the place.*

But he wasn't awake.

I decided science was wrong, and Grandma McShane was at least partly right. There had to be something else. Some other place dead people went. Something that explained those creepy feelings I had that we weren't alone.

Eventually, I fell asleep and dreamed I was flying through space. Over my shoulder, the Earth got smaller and smaller until it disappeared in the stars. It wasn't scary, but it wasn't exactly a good dream, either—mostly it just felt lonely.

CHAPTER EIGHT

THE THIRTEENTH-FLOOR ELEVATOR

MOM TOLD US we couldn't explore empty apartments, but she didn't say anything about the rest of the building. By late morning I was so tired of being in our lame apartment that I decided to go exploring again. Mal didn't take as much convincing as I expected: He still wanted to finish *Minecraft* Brunhild Tower and there were more parts of the real Brunhild Tower he needed to see.

First, we went up. The elevator lobbies in each tier were connected by fire stairs, so we went to the top floor and walked down, opening the fire doors on each landing and peeking in. Each one was completely different. Some looked rich, with thick rugs, leather benches, coat racks, and umbrella stands. Others just had flimsy tables holding junk mail and petrified hard candy. But most of the elevator lobbies were empty—just dusty little rooms.

We tiptoed and shushed each other when we started out, trying to be sneaky, but we never heard or saw anyone to hide from, so eventually we walked, talked, and tried to step on each other's toes without worrying about anyone seeing or hearing us.

On the first floor, behind the lobby, there were service hallways that led to the laundry room, the package room, the freight elevators for all three tiers, and a weird door by the back loading dock. Someone must have lived there, judging by the doorbell and welcome mat, but Mal and I couldn't imagine who would want to walk out their front door into a loading dock.

We also found an open door that led to an empty indoor pool, with changing rooms and a sauna and even a hot tub, all covered with so much dust you could practically swim in it. I don't think it had been used in a hundred years—it looked like a museum of swimming.

"I can't believe this place has a pool!" said Mal.

"I can't believe it's empty," I moaned.

We also discovered the basement, which was huge and kind of spooky. We decided it was okay to try doors down there, since none of them looked like apartments. Most were locked, but the ones that weren't led to a workshop, the two-level garage, and a huge maze of storage lockers. The lockers were basically wooden closets that went on row after row after row, and most of them had padlocks on the doors. We snooped in the ones that weren't locked but didn't find anything besides mummified suitcases and sagging cardboard boxes.

Mal, of course, had been carrying his clipboard the

whole time, sketching diagrams and making notes while I led the way.

"What time is it?" he asked.

I pretended to look at my wrist. "Hair past a mole."

That was one of Dad's corny jokes and, since his watch was in my pillowcase, as close as I got to knowing the real time.

"Last time I heard that one, I laughed so hard I fell off my dinosaur and broke my wooden underpants," said Mal.

Also one of Dad's jokes. Look, I never said they were any good. The jokes he told and the songs he sang all seemed a hundred years old. Most of the songs seemed to be about whales or whiskey.

"Well, I'm hungry," said Mal.

I realized I was, too. We took the stairs back up to the lobby and got in the elevator. I reached for the *14* button and froze, my finger an inch away from the panel.

"What are you waiting for, Colm?" asked Mal.

He stopped short when he saw it, too.

Immediately under the *14*, there was now a button for the thirteenth floor.

"But . . . but . . . ," Mal said, not finishing his sentence, because even without telepathy we both knew the end of that sentence was *THERE'S NO THIRTEENTH FLOOR IN THIS BUILDING!*

"I think I'm hallucinating," I said.

"You can't be hallucinating," said Mal, "because I see it, too. There's no such thing as a joint hallucination."

"Maybe there is for twins?"

"Whatever you do, don't push it . . . just in case it's real," he whispered.

Seeing the button gave me a feeling of creepy-crawly dread, like watching a stuffed animal suddenly sit up. I didn't want to push the button because I didn't know what would happen.

On the other hand, the fact that Mal was afraid of what would happen really made me want to do it.

So I pushed the button.

"COLM!" yelped Mal as the elevator doors closed.

Once we started to climb, Mal began hyperventilating.

"What if it . . . what if it really stops on the thirteenth floor?"

"Well, wouldn't that technically be *our* floor?" I asked.

"Then what's on fourteen?"

I didn't know the answer, but at least Mal was freaked out, which meant I could enjoy his fear instead of worrying about what would happen when—

The elevator stopped. The doors slid open, and the bell went *DING*, a nice clear chime, not the muted *TINK* we'd gotten used to.

The elevator lobby in front of us looked a lot like ours . . . except it was completely different. There were framed drawings of birds on the walls, which were covered in a dizzy pattern of silver-and-blue wallpaper, and the light bulbs in the little chandelier looked like something a museum would have used to explain how Thomas Edison invented electricity.

The little room didn't just look weird—it *felt* weird,

like the air itself was crackling with an energy that hummed in my brain. And every time I looked at the walls, I could have sworn they were in a slightly different place, even though I didn't actually see them move.

Maybe it was just the wallpaper.

"Let's go back," whimpered Mal.

I shook my head, my heartbeat sounding like a pair of sneakers in a washing machine. "Let's go in," I said.

The elevator door chimed again and started to close, but I put my hand out and stopped it. Taking a deep breath, I stepped halfway out.

Suddenly, from the door on the left, I heard voices!

"*So I'm the annoying one, am I?*" said a woman's voice in a sarcastic tone.

"*Well, I'm not the one whose nose whistles in my sleep!*" shouted a man.

"*My nose whistles? Well, your snores sound like the State Street Subway!*"

"*Give it a rest, you two,*" said a deeper man's voice.

"*Where's my hat?*" asked the first man.

"*Oh, that's right, go down to the lobby and play cribbage with your pals,*" said the woman. "*That's your answer for everything!*"

I heard the bolt snap back on the door. I jumped into the elevator and hammered the *DOOR CLOSE* and *L* buttons like I was typing a hundred words per minute with one finger. Mal slid down into the corner and pulled his knees against his chest.

The doorknob turned, and the heavy door creaked open. Finally, the elevator started to close.

"Wait! Hold the elevator!" said the first man's voice.

I stumbled back, thumping into the wall of the car just as the doors finally, mercifully slid shut.

Neither of us said a word while the elevator dropped to the lobby. Without even discussing it—making me wonder if Mal was finally starting to give in to telepathy—we both headed straight for the front door.

Before we got there, though, we literally ran into the Princess, making her drop the stack of mail she was holding. Today she was wearing emerald green from head to toe and carrying a purse that looked like it was made out of an armadillo.

"Vot did I say about goink out at lunchtime?" she asked as we got down on hands and knees to pick up the scattered envelopes.

I looked at Mal, who was supposed to remember things for both of us, but he just stared. I think he was still in shock.

"Not to do it?" I guessed.

"Exactly so," said the Princess, her eyes flashing. "Und I remind you: Brunhild Tower ees not your playground."

We gave her mail back and hurried out, Virgilio holding the door open for us, then run-walked down the sidewalk. I think we both wanted to get as far away from the building as possible. And since Brunhild Tower took up most of the block, that meant crossing the street, even though Mom told us not to.

We went two blocks and crossed again to a pedestrian tunnel under Lake Shore Drive. The tunnel let out in a little sunken park that a sign called the Peace Garden, where there was a man-made waterfall that splashed into a pool and a statue of two kids fighting over a ball.

Everything in the park except the statue—the waterfall, the pool, the terraced walls of its garden—was made of different-sized rocks cemented together. There were even stone benches. Mal and I sat on one of them and stared at the falling water. It made a nice sound but was almost drowned out by the traffic zooming by above us.

"What just happened?" I asked.

"Maybe we had simultaneous visual and auditory hallucinations," said Mal.

He looked like he'd seen a ghost, and maybe we almost had. The thing that makes Mal different from most kids is that, with most kids, if you told them Santa Claus was real, they'd be psyched. But Mal would be terrified because it wasn't something he could explain with facts. I was scared, too, but I was also excited. Maybe ghosts *were* real.

"That's not what happened and you know it," I said.

"But what did?" he asked. "And what do we tell Mom?"

The bushes behind us rustled, a few clods of dirt fell on our arms and knees, and all of a sudden, Tamika dropped down onto the bench between us.

"Tell Mom what?" she asked.

CHAPTER NINE

NOT TELLING MOM

"OKAY, NOW I *know* you're following us," I told Tamika.

"I am NOT," she said. "For your information, you're sitting on my reading bench."

She was holding a book, it was true, but that still didn't explain why she'd mysteriously appeared from the bushes.

"For all we know, you just grabbed that book from the Little Free Library across the street so you'd have an excuse for following us," Mal surprised me by saying.

Tamika rolled her eyes. "You should seriously see someone about your paranoia problem. I read on this bench every day, and the bookmark shows you I'm on chapter eight, so there's no way I picked up this book just now. What don't you want to tell your mom?"

"None of your business," I said.

"Did you do something you weren't supposed to? Were you snooping around the Princess's apartment again?"

"Why can't you read on that bench over there?" I asked, pointing to an identical one on the other side of the fountain.

"Because this is where I always read."

I stood up and Mal did, too. It wasn't worth arguing over who got to sit where.

"Why should we tell you, anyway?" Mal asked.

"Because I can keep a secret." Tamika pretended to zip her lips. "Also, I'm super knowledgeable because I've read one thousand six hundred and ninety-seven books, many of them nonfiction."

"Thanks for the offer," I said. "We'll discuss it and get back to you."

She stood up, looking like she was thinking about following us. "So you're both named Malcolm? Can I call you Malcolm One and Malcolm Two?"

Of course she remembered Mal's screwup from when we first met her. "I'm Colm, and he's Mal," I said. "Sometimes our mom calls us Malcolm to save time, but she's the only one who does that."

"What grade will you be in?" she asked.

"Seventh," said Mal as I grabbed his arm and pulled him toward the tunnel.

"When you're ready to tell me your secret, I live in 302," Tamika called.

We walked back under Lake Shore Drive through the tunnel, which someone had painted with a mural of a bunch of random stuff. Cars whizzed over our heads.

"There's no way we're telling Tamika," said Mal. "But I think we should tell Mom."

"Maybe we should tell Tamika," I said. "After all,

she's lived in Brunhild Tower for a while; she might know something about the thirteenth floor. But we're definitely not telling Mom."

"I know what you're thinking," said Mal as we crossed the street and headed back home.

I wanted to tell him he didn't, but unfortunately, he did. After Dad died, things were pretty messed up—I guess you could say that I was pretty messed up. I did a lot of stuff without knowing why I was doing it, and one of the biggest things I did was tell lies. We stayed home from school a long time after the funeral, and when we finally went back, I had a hard time with everything: raising my hand in class, talking to other kids, even running laps in gym. Everyone was nice and understanding until they weren't anymore, like they forgot my dad had died. But that was all I could think about.

And so I started making up reasons why I didn't do my homework or why I didn't feel like running laps around the gym. At first they were little lies, like saying my grandparents were visiting or I had a stomachache. But after I used up those lies, I made up bigger ones, and I wasn't even using them as excuses anymore. I told the gym teacher it was José Aguilar who had kicked all the soccer balls onto the school roof, even though I didn't know who did it. I also spread the rumor that Ms. Richards used to be a spokesmodel on a TV shopping network, just because I'd seen someone who kind of looked like her. And I told the assistant principal that, on weekends, I earned money for our family by hanging out in the parking lot at the hardware store until I got hired onto yard crews.

Yeah, I got in a lot of trouble for lying. Mom made me see a therapist named Dr. Raymond, who had a bristly beard, wore jeans, and kept telling me it was okay if I felt like crying. I never cried in front of him, but I eventually stopped lying so much. Dr. Raymond told me feelings are complicated, and sometimes we do bad stuff when we don't want to think about bad things, and sometimes we draw attention to ourselves "accidentally on purpose." Like, we might think we want everybody to leave us alone, but we secretly don't.

So you can see why I couldn't tell Mom that our building had a floor that magically appeared and disappeared.

Brunhild Tower stood above my brother and me like a cliff. If I craned my neck, I could see our windows on the corner of the real-life thirteenth floor. The apartment next door didn't have any drapes or shades, and neither did the ones above or below.

"Well, I'm glad you know what I'm thinking, Mal," I said. "Not only will she think I'm lying, she'll think I'm getting you to lie now, too, and we'll both have to go see Dr. Raymond."

"Dr. Raymond is in Dallas."

"They have therapists in Chicago, Mal."

"Well, you might be full of crap, but Mom knows she can always believe me, so I'm going to tell her."

I hauled back my arm, ready to hit him so hard he'd get bruises on both sides—but suddenly there was Virgilio, holding the door open for us.

"Welcome home, gentlemen," he said with a big smile.

• • •

When we sat down for dinner, Mal and I both had our game faces on. He was ready to tell, and I was determined to keep him from telling by any means necessary. My plan was to get Mom talking, and keep her talking, by asking about her day. But I also had to avoid rookie mistakes, like asking more than one question at once.

"So how was work, Mom?" I asked as soon as she sat down.

She looked exhausted. I probably could have guessed how she was feeling since dinner was fried chicken, mashed potatoes, and coleslaw, all served from a greasy paper bag.

While Mal and I started gnawing on drumsticks, she took the skin off a breast and started slicing it with a knife and fork. You probably remember how she eats her spaghetti.

"Oh, fine. How was your day?"

Mal's eyebrows went up. She had just given him his opening, and he would have pounced on it—if he hadn't just taken a big bite of chicken.

My mouth was full, too, so I chewed furiously, while a new thought occurred to me: *Mom* was lying. It was obvious from her tired face and slumped shoulders that her day wasn't "fine." While I gulped my half-chewed chicken and washed it down with a swallow of milk, I decided to go on the offensive.

"It doesn't look like your day was fine, Mom," I blurted before Mal could get his mouth open.

Looking surprised, she put her knife and fork down. "I guess I'm not as good at faking as I thought I was," she said. "You're right, Colm. I'm having a hard time learning how they do things. I still haven't seen Professor Parker, but I'm actually assisting *all* the professors in sociology. Vonetta, the department chair, had me spend the whole day updating schedules and calendars for the coming year and then told me I hadn't formatted them the way she prefers. I can't say she's wrong to be so demanding, but I wish she would be more patient."

I wasn't sure what to say to that—and neither was Mal. We didn't have to read each other's minds because our faces were clear enough.

Mom gave a little laugh that wasn't very convincing and reached out to touch both of us on our arms. "I don't want you to worry. New jobs and new places have their challenges. It's just been so long that I've forgotten what it's like to learn a new routine."

Mal picked up his drumstick again and started

nibbling. With Mom having a lot on her mind, I guessed he didn't want to add to her worries by telling her what we'd seen that day.

I put my drumstick down and stared at it. I wasn't hungry anymore. Now the greasy food reminded me of being stuck in the van with my duffel bag under my feet and Eric's carrier between me and Mal. What we'd seen and what Mal might say suddenly didn't seem so important. What if Mom's new job didn't work out and we had to move again?

Would Dad's voice start to fade away?

CHAPTER TEN

WATCHING THE PROFESSOR

THE NEXT DAY, Mal and I avoided each other. Mal worked on *Minecraft* Brunhild Tower, clicking his mouse nonstop while he stared at the screen. Sometimes I used to think that if he could leave the real world to live in Malandia, he would.

I was tempted to log in from Mom's laptop and make problems for him, like replacing all the floors with lava or filling the rooms with cows, but decided I didn't want to deal with him in the real world or the virtual world. How can two kids look exactly the same and still be totally different?

Bored with *Kart Krashers*, I played a few other games, watched some TV, and even tried to read a book—but I couldn't get into it and the musty smell of the couch was starting to bother me.

I gave up. After a peanut-butter-and-banana sandwich for lunch, I left the apartment and rode the elevator down to the lobby on my own. Then, instead of getting out when the doors opened and the bell went *TINK*, I rode it up to the seventeenth floor, staring at the control panel the whole way. The buttons lit up one by one: *11*, *12*, *14*, *15*.

At the top, I got out and took the stairs down. The stairwell looked like it hadn't been painted since the building was built. Low-wattage light bulbs showed pipes, wiring, old fire hoses, mousetraps, and floor numbers painted on every door. Going from top to bottom, fourteen was followed by twelve.

I stopped in between, where a concrete slab formed the floor of the fourteenth floor and the ceiling of the twelfth. It was strange how calling the thirteenth floor the fourteenth made everyone think about it differently, like there really was a floor missing between it and the one below.

How could a new floor of the building have appeared yesterday? Would it happen again?

I went down and down, all the way to the first floor, where I left the dusty old stairwell to head outside. I needed some fresh air.

As I neared the front doors, Professor Parker was signing the visitors' book at the desk. When he saw me, he put down the pen and turned, his big body and two canes blocking my way.

"And which one are you? Colm?"

It was probably just luck, but the fact that he guessed right bothered me. I nodded and waited for him to get out of the way. Behind him, Virgilio stepped to the outer door, ready to let me out.

But the Professor wasn't done with me yet. "How do you like your new home?" he asked, his rumbling voice starting deep in his chest.

"Pretty good, I guess," I said.

"Have you met any of your neighbors?"

"I met a girl named Tamika. And I met the Princess, too."

The Professor leaned in, wobbling on his canes like it took all his strength to stay upright. His white beard had yellow patches, his teeth were crooked, his left eye was milky white—and the pipe sticking out of his pocket explained the way he smelled.

"And what did you think of the Princess?" he asked.

Eccentric. Annoying. Crazy. Lots of words came to mind, but it didn't seem right to say them to someone who weirded me out even more than she did. So I shrugged.

"She's okay, I guess," I said.

The Professor brought his big, shaggy head even closer. He lowered his voice. "Listen to me, Colm McShane: Princess Veronica is not to be trusted."

"Okay," I said, because I didn't know how else to answer. It wasn't as if the Princess had asked me to trust her or anything. In the future, I planned to avoid both the Professor *and* the Princess. And why wasn't he at work, anyway?

He stayed there a second longer than he needed to, looking at me with his good eye. Then he smiled and caned his way to the inner door.

Virgilio let go of the outer door, said "Excuse me" to me, and opened the inner door for the Professor, who clomped into the building, the smell of smoke leaking out of his clothes. Even though it must have been eighty-five degrees outside, he was wearing a sweater and a corduroy jacket.

Just then, the phone rang. Virgilio answered it, holding up a finger to let me know he'd just be a moment. I could have opened the door myself, but Mom had told me to let the doormen do their job, so I just stood there waiting and feeling kind of dumb.

Behind the desk were six vertical indicators to show which floor each of the elevators was on. While Virgilio explained to the caller that she had reached the wrong number—Brunhild Tower was not a funeral home—the 03-04 passenger elevator started to rise. Its arrow went straight up, past ten, eleven, and twelve—and stopped halfway to fourteen!

I looked at the clock on the wall. It was 1:04.

Suddenly, my heart started racing.

Virgilio hung up the phone, laughed, and went to open the door for me. But now I didn't want to go outside.

"Sorry, I forgot something," I told him. "I need to go back in."

He shrugged and opened the inner door again. I went through to the lobby and turned left into our hall.

In the corner opposite the 03-04 elevator was a giant vase almost as tall as I was, with leafy vines spilling out of the top. I pushed the elevator button and then hid behind the vase while the elevator car came down.

When the doors opened, it was empty.

Cautiously, I left my hiding place and went inside the elevator. On the control panel, the *13* button was there, looking just as real as the rest of the buttons. Across the hall, sunlight streamed in through the tall windows. It was daytime and I wasn't dreaming.

Taking a deep breath, I pushed the button.

When the doors opened on the thirteenth floor, I felt the same electric charge as before. Everything looked the same: the wallpaper, the light bulbs, the floor. I didn't hear any voices, but that didn't stop me from pounding the lobby button like a woodpecker making a hole in a telephone pole.

On the first floor, I practically exploded out of the elevator and sprinted to my hiding place behind the vase. The Professor was obviously visiting the thirteenth floor. He had gone up, and in, and he hadn't come out. I planned to watch and wait until he did.

What was he doing up there?

I didn't find out anytime soon. And while I bided my time, my biggest problems were finding a comfortable position and not sneezing. The leaves on the vines hanging down the sides of the vase were dusty and, I realized eventually, totally fake. When I fluffed them up to improve the camouflage, dust rose in a cloud.

For a big building, it sure was quiet. It was hard to tell how much time was passing, but I only saw one person go by: a little old man wearing slippers and suspenders who whistled his way to the mailroom and back.

When the arrow on the elevator indicator finally moved again, I almost missed it: It went up a half tick to fourteen, paused, then slowly began to come down.

That was interesting.

The Professor made his way out of the elevator deliberately, making sure his feet and canes were carefully placed before he put any weight on them. Passing my hiding place, he stopped and sniffed—and my heart stuttered, thinking he was *smelling* me—then pulled an old cloth handkerchief out of his pocket and had a long, wet blow.

It must have been the dust.

Behind him, at the very end of the long hall, the 01-02 elevator doors slid open and Tamika came out, carrying a book. She walked closer, watching the Professor clomp away—I heard him thank Virgilio as the lobby doors swung shut—and then came directly over to the vase.

I thought I was practically invisible, but Tamika walked straight up and asked, "Are you Mal or Colm? Why are you hiding?"

"It's Colm, and I'm not hiding," I said. "I'm just . . . hanging out."

"Does it have something to do with the thing you can't tell your mom?"

I was starting to wonder if somehow I was related to Tamika because she was better at twin telepathy than Mal.

Instead of answering, I pushed the dusty fake vines aside and crawled out from behind the vase.

"Do you want to come to my place and hang out?" asked Tamika.

I did, but I said I didn't—sometimes my brain works like that.

"Then can I come to your place?" she asked without missing a beat.

"I guess so," I said.

The elevator still smelled like old pipe smoke from the Professor's clothes.

"Hey, have you ever noticed—" I started to say as I reached for the control panel to push the button for my floor, seeing at the same time that the *13* button had disappeared again.

"Noticed what?" asked Tamika.

"Oh, nothing," I said, my mind racing as fast as the motorcycles that screamed down Lake Shore Drive at night.

CHAPTER ELEVEN

MAL IS A JERK

TAMIKA WALKED INTO our apartment like she owned the place. I followed her in, thinking about how the thirteenth-floor button only appeared from one to two o'clock—the hour the Princess had warned us to stay home. During that time, the Professor had been visiting the thirteenth floor. But who was he visiting? And why?

"Hey, Mal," said Tamika, poking her head into the dining room.

Mal was so surprised to see her that all he could do was offer a bug-eyed "Hi, Tamika" as he looked up from the computer. I wished he would have been doing something embarrassing, like picking his nose or scratching his butt. Unfortunately, the only embarrassing thing he was doing was being himself, but Tamika didn't know him well enough to understand that yet.

She kept moving, snooping her way through the apartment until she ended up in the living room.

"All your furniture is so *old*," she said, scratching Eric behind the ears and wrinkling her nose at the way the couch smelled.

"It's not ours," I explained. "It came with the place. The previous renters left some other stuff, too."

I took her to the little room off the kitchen and showed her where we were piling everything until Mom had time to take it to the Salvation Army. Tamika sat down on the floor and started looking through it, immediately finding one of the notebooks with the name *Teddy* on the front.

"Did you ever know someone named Teddy in this building?" I asked.

She shook her head, paging through the notebook. "No, but see how old this is. It looks like an antique." She stopped and pointed to a date. "March 17, 1933—it's more than eighty years old!"

Now it was my turn to shake my head. "This apartment must have been empty for a really long time."

Tamika put the notebook down and picked through the other left-behind things. "I don't know. All this stuff looks like it's from different decades. This wall sculpture looks like something from my grandparents' house, and this boom box is so old it takes cassette tapes."

"So you never knew anyone who lived in this apartment?"

"Nope," she said, dusting off her hands and standing

up. "I used to do chores for Mrs. Gillard down in 704, but I've never been in this one."

I followed her back into the dining room, where she peppered Mal with questions about *Minecraft*, and Malandia, and why he was building a virtual Brunhild Tower, until he gave up and closed his browser because she obviously wasn't going to let him get any work done.

"So, do you ever read books, or do you just sit in front of a computer all day?" Tamika asked him.

"I like to read," he said, embarrassed. "All kinds of stuff."

Unfortunately, that was true: As much as he loved *Minecraft*, Mal had always been more of a reader than me. He and Tamika started talking about their favorite books. Mal was mainly into fantasy, and Tamika liked historical fiction, books about scientists, and anything about Chicago.

"Do you just read books all day, or do you ever do anything else, like play with friends?" I asked Tamika, annoyed that I was left out.

"Are you suggesting there's anything wrong with reading books all day?" she said defensively. "For your information, most of my friends are at day camp, and my best friend, Binita, is at sleepaway camp in Michigan."

Turning to Mal, she told him about another book she liked, and before I knew it they were having their own little book club right there in the dining room.

I was the one who invited Tamika—well, I agreed to let her come up after she invited herself, anyway—but all of a sudden she was acting like Mal's best friend. It was just like the time back in Dallas when I invited Ben to play basketball and then he spent the whole afternoon playing *Minecraft* with Mal.

I'm not sure either of them even noticed when I left and went back to the living room, where Eric was now lying on his back in a sunbeam, baking himself like a furry casserole. I scratched his belly slowly so he wouldn't latch on with his claws and start rabbit-kicking me.

What *was* the deal with the thirteenth floor, and whose voices had we heard there? And were the people the Professor was visiting alive?

Maybe the thirteenth floor was some kind of portal to the afterlife, and everyone who lived there was . . . dead.

And if that was true, maybe you could visit dead people and come back.

Even though it was another hot summer afternoon, I started having those shivery, late-night feelings again. It creeped me out, so before I got all the way to the empty-universe endless-starry-sky thing, I went back to the dining room to see if Mal and Tamika were done talking about books.

When I walked in, they were laughing about something, and when I said, "What are you laughing about?" it only made them laugh more.

So I asked, "Was Mal telling you about the time everyone in music class turned around and he had the ends of the drumsticks in his nostrils?"

That made Mal stop laughing, all right. He turned bright red as Tamika cracked up even harder. She had a nice laugh, like she didn't care how loud she was.

"No way!" she said.

Mal counterattacked. "Well, I'm guessing Colm hasn't told you about the time at our old apartment when he went out into the hallway to get the paper and the door locked behind him—and he was only wearing his underwear."

I couldn't believe he told her that story. First of all, I only went out to get the paper because he wouldn't stop whining about wanting to do the sudoku, and even though I wouldn't have minded reading the comics he made us decide who'd do it by playing rock-paper-scissors, which I lost. Sure, I should have put on some pants, but he wouldn't open the door to let me back in!

Tamika was really cracking up now.

"You guys are hilarious," she said. "Are you like this all the time?"

"Actually, he's usually even more of a jerk," I said.

"I wish I had a twin sister," said Tamika, sounding like she actually meant it.

"Believe me, you don't," said Mal.

"You're both *really* different. I mean, you *look* exactly the same, but obviously you have different personalities."

"*Obviously,*" I said, trying desperately to think of another embarrassing fact about Mal and getting ready to make one up.

"But how do people tell you apart?" asked Tamika.

Mal grinned and sat down across from her at the dining room table. "It's easy: All you have to do is compare our report cards."

"*Mal,*" I warned him.

Tamika winced, like she thought he'd gone too far, but then she laughed, like she couldn't help it.

"I'm the one who gets straight As," said Mal, just to make sure she got the point.

"And what do you get, Colm?" asked Tamika.

I didn't have anything funny to say, and I was so mad I couldn't even think of a good comeback. So what I *got* was out of there, stomping to our room and slamming the door so hard I'm surprised the pictures didn't fall off the wall.

Having a twin brother is like having a pebble in your shoe. Sometimes it's just annoying and you can kind of ignore it. But then all of a sudden it stings your foot so hard your eyes water, and the only thing you can do is take your shoe off and shake out the pebble.

Staring out the window at the endless blue of Lake Michigan and the surging cars on Lake Shore Drive, I eventually came up with a plan for revenge.

Unfortunately, it would have to wait until the next day.

CHAPTER TWELVE

REVENGE

FOR MY PLAN to work, Mal couldn't suspect I was still mad at him, so I spent the morning pretending everything was fine. I watched him working on *Minecraft* Brunhild Tower in Malandia and acted interested when he told me how he was able to figure out what the other apartments looked like by searching rental listings online.

"There are a *ton* of apartments for rent in this building, Colm," he told me excitedly, probably thinking I had forgotten all about what a jerk he was the day before. "Some of them have floor plans, so I've been able to figure out what all six apartment styles look like. And after completing one whole floor, I can just stack fifteen of them on top of the lobby."

Actually, sixteen, I thought. *One more for the phantom floor that shows up every day.*

He was doing a decent job and had even started decorating some of the apartments. Ours looked like our real one, and the Princess's was filled with bookshelves and dozens of cats.

After lunch, I started trying to drag him out of the apartment, but he didn't want to go.

"I want to finish this part first," he said.

But as soon as he completed one *Minecraft* apartment, he wanted to start on another. The clock was ticking—and time was running out.

Finally, I said, "Look, Mal. While you've been playing on the computer, I discovered something important about the thirteenth floor."

That got his attention. Mal looked up and pushed his hair out of his eyes. "What is it?"

I pushed my hair out of mine. "I can't just tell you. You have to see it in person."

He looked skeptical, but I guess he believed me because he got up and put his shoes on.

He was going so slowly that it was all I could do to keep myself from dragging him out the door. Based on the clock I'd seen in the corner of his computer screen, I guessed there were only a few minutes left by the time we made it to the elevator.

"The button is there again," Mal whispered when he saw it, like he hadn't believed it was true.

"Of course it's there," I said impatiently. "It's there every day between one and two, and you would have known that if you weren't so obsessed with *Minecraft*."

I pushed *13*, and the doors closed. It was a short ride. We went down one floor, and the doors opened with a *DING* onto the silver-and-blue wallpaper, the old-fashioned light bulbs, and the atmosphere that felt like an approaching electrical storm.

Mal looked scared. "What did you want to show me?"

I stepped behind him and pressed the *DOOR CLOSE* button. Then, as the doors started to move toward each other, I gave him a huge shove that sent him stumbling into the thirteenth-floor elevator lobby.

"THIS!" I yelled.

He spun around, white as a sheet.

"Who's the stupid one now?" I taunted him as the doors slid shut.

Laughing to myself, I leaned against the far side of the elevator, folded my arms, and waited for him to open the doors. Being nice to him all morning had been completely worth it to scare the heck out of him. Now we were even.

The elevator didn't move. A minute passed, and the doors didn't open. Then another. After one more minute, I started to wonder if Mal had gotten over being scared and decided to go exploring.

I didn't want to miss that!

I pressed *DOOR OPEN*, and the doors parted with a *TINK*—onto the fourteenth floor and our elevator lobby. There was the table, the lamp, and the four black-and-white pictures of Chicago. I hadn't even felt the elevator move.

I reached out to press the button for *13*, but it was gone.

• • •

I felt dizzy. My knees wobbled. As the doors slid shut again, I pressed the button for the lobby, needing to get out of this crazy building so I could think.

Crap! I only wanted to scare Mal as payback for making me look stupid in front of Tamika. I never meant to trap him in another dimension—or wherever he was now. It was his own fault for taking so long that we didn't leave the apartment until almost two o'clock.

It might have been a little bit my fault, too, but I wasn't going to dwell on that. Right now, I had a big, big problem. And as much as I hated to admit it, part of the problem was that my brainiac brother wasn't there to help me figure out how to rescue him. Mal was probably going to be stuck on the thirteenth floor for the next twenty-three hours, and I had to keep Mom from finding out, too.

When I left the building, Virgilio said, "Have a good day—now, is it Mal or Colm?" and I felt so guilty I didn't even want to say my name, so I just mumbled and kept going.

Even though I wasn't sure I wanted to explain to her what was happening, I half hoped I'd run into Tamika, but she wasn't in the Peace Garden on her usual reading bench, and she wasn't lurking in the bushes behind it, either. I kept walking the way we had with Mom—past the Little Free Library to the school, around the back of the school to the playground, and then down the street with the mansions—but my thoughts were still jumbled and I had no better idea what to do next.

I didn't know another soul in Chicago besides Tamika, the Princess, the Professor, Virgilio, and Dante. Actually, I realized, the Princess was probably the best person to ask for help. It couldn't have been a coincidence that she told us to stay home each day during the exact time the thirteenth floor appeared—she had to know something.

When I got back to the building, Virgilio stirred the air with his finger and then pointed at me. "I figured it out: You're Mal."

"Uh . . . how did you guess?" I asked.

He grinned triumphantly. "Well, you just looked deep in thought, like you often do. Colm always seems so happy-go-lucky."

I shook my head like I couldn't believe how smart he was, but really I was glad he guessed wrong—I needed people to think Mal wasn't missing, and Virgilio was already helping with that story.

After Virgilio let me in, I passed the 03-04 elevator and walked down the long south hall to the 01-02 elevator. I rode it all the way to the top and, taking a deep breath, knocked at 1701.

There was no answer. Pressing my ear against the door and holding my breath, I could just make out what sounded like . . . purring?

A fuzzy calico paw reached under the door and playfully batted at my shoelace.

I knocked again, only then remembering that the

Princess had said to have Dante call up before visiting. But why Dante? He wasn't even on duty.

It was time to try Tamika. She was just as much of a know-it-all as my brother, after all—hopefully she knew something useful. I just wouldn't tell her she was part of the reason Mal was stuck in another dimension.

I went down to the third floor. There was a nameplate that said *Jackson* over 302. After I knocked, I heard footsteps, then saw the light in the peephole darken while somebody looked through. Then Tamika opened the door. Naturally, she was holding a book.

"Colm?" she said.

"How'd you know?" I asked.

"Lucky guess. I think your voice is a little bit different, now that I hear you speak. Do you want to come in?"

"You're not going to believe what I'm about to tell you," I said.

Tamika held up the book. "I'm reading a book about scientists who used themselves as guinea pigs for their own experiments—sometimes with fatal results. So I doubt it's weirder than that."

I stepped past her into her apartment. "Trust me, it is."

• • •

"That's the most preposterous thing I've ever heard," said Tamika after I'd finished telling her what happened to Mal.

We were sitting on the couch in her living room,

where the furniture looked like it belonged to her family, not some random strangers from a long time ago.

"Well, it happens to be true," I said. "Haven't you ever noticed a button for the thirteenth floor?"

She shook her head. "No, but then again, I'm on a much lower floor. And I've lived here my whole life, so I press the button without really looking, anyway." Pausing, she squinted skeptically at me. "You do realize that what you're saying defies all the laws of science, not to mention plain old common sense?"

"I didn't make those laws, and I'm not the one breaking them, either," I said, frustrated. "Isn't it possible there are some things even scientists don't know?"

"I think you're messing with me. Actually, you're probably Mal, and Colm put you up to this, and he's going to jump out and say *boo* when we go looking for him."

Suddenly, I felt so tired that I just wanted to lie down on the floor and quit right then and there. Instead, I stood up. "Well, thanks for nothing," I said as I headed for the door.

Tamika beat me there—maybe because I was walking as slow as Dante—and planted herself in front of it. The look on her face gave me hope. It was—I don't know—nice.

"This is for real?" she asked quietly.

"With the world as my witness," I said. "You can look everywhere for Mal, but you're not going to find him until tomorrow at one p.m.—and only hopefully then. I don't even know if he's okay. I blew it big-time, but right now I need a way to hide the truth from my mom until I can bring him back."

Tamika looked me in the eye. "So you're going to go into the thirteenth floor tomorrow?"

I shrugged. "I don't think I have a choice."

She nodded and pushed off from the door. "All right. I'll help you stall your mom. But I'm also coming on the rescue. If the thirteenth floor is real, I want to see it for myself."

"Deal," I told her. If she wanted to risk life, limb, and the possibility of being lost forever in another dimension, that was fine by me.

"Let me make a phone call," she said.

While Tamika went to use the phone, I went back inside the apartment and looked around. The Jacksons' place was a lot nicer than ours and more modern than anything I'd seen in Brunhild Tower. It had wall-to-wall carpeting, polished wood furniture, and cream-colored couches my own mom would never have trusted me to sit on. Nothing looked expensive, but everything was put away neatly and it looked like a real home.

I heard Tamika's voice in the kitchen, rising and falling, punctuated by some yeses and nos. I was tempted to go down the hall and see what her room looked like, but fortunately I didn't because all of a sudden she came back.

"I've got it all figured out," she said. "You and Mal are coming over for dinner."

CHAPTER FOURTEEN

JAZZ AT THE JACKSONS'

LIKE MAL, TAMIKA was good at problem solving and planning ahead—I'm better at thinking on my feet. As much as I hated to admit it, I could see why they got along.

After she explained the details of her plan, I went back home, where the apartment felt huge and empty without Mal. He may have been a jerk, but he belonged in the real world, not another dimension. My footsteps echoed off the wooden floors and high ceilings, making me even more lonely, so I took my shoes off and walked around in my socks.

I was full of nervous energy and wanted to do something right away, but unfortunately I had to kill some time until Mom got home. I knew all of Mal's logins—even though he didn't know I knew—so I decided to visit Malandia until then. Since Mal wasn't around to stop me, I promised myself I wouldn't mess with anything. A few keystrokes and I was in.

Malandia was huge: Mal had been working on it for more than three years, and he never got rid of anything. I saw the first village he built, with simple square houses made out of brick and wood. I flew over the maze he'd designed and filled with groaning zombies. Between the Mount Olympus he'd made for his class project on Greek myths and an amusement park with a dozen different roller coasters, I saw something I'd never noticed: our old apartment building. It was nothing like Brunhild Tower, of course, just a four-story box made out of white bricks, but through the windows I could see he'd made a tiny apartment just like the one we used to live in. Our bunk beds were there, and so was the coffee table where we ate pizza every Friday night. I hadn't seen him working on it in Chicago, so he must have built it before we left Dallas. Maybe he was worried he'd forget.

Suddenly, I missed Dallas, and Dad, and Mom—and even Mal. I moved on before my eyes started leaking.

In the distance, I could see a building that looked exactly like Brunhild Tower. As I got closer, I could see how carefully he'd designed the outside. It wasn't an exact replica, of course, because he had to build everything out of blocks that were all the same size, but it was pretty good. He'd even filled in the parking lot, some of Lake Shore Drive, and the parks across the street.

I went in the front door, through the vestibule, and into the lobby. Working elevators are hard to build in *Minecraft*, even for a genius like Mal, so the elevator was just an empty shaft I flew up until I reached the fourteenth floor. Our apartment looked pretty much like it did in real life.

Now, if it were me, I wouldn't have bothered making everything so realistic. The whole point of *Minecraft* is that it's *not* real; you get to play with redstone, lava, TNT, and other awesome stuff. I would have filled the swimming pool with squid, planted grass on the roof, and blinged out the walls of our apartment with precious minerals. Instead of windows, I would have built glass walls, and I would have added a balcony so I could look out over my kingdom. But Mal stuck to the facts, and our apartment in *Minecraft* Brunhild Tower was every bit as boring as our apartment in the real-world Brunhild Tower.

What did it look like where he was now? Were the people there nice, and was he safe, or was he running for his life? I also wondered if he had his notebook with him so he could draw what he saw and add a floor to his *Minecraft* Brunhild Tower when he came back.

If we could get him back.

If we both suddenly disappeared forever, poor Mom would be all alone.

A meowing cat came into the *Minecraft* living room at the same time Eric started rubbing against my legs, which was a strange coincidence. I reached down to give Eric's chin a scratch. Real-life cats were definitely better than virtual ones.

I guess I lost track of time, because when I heard Mom's key in the lock I was totally unprepared.

I called Tamika and let it ring two times, which was our signal. Then I hung up and raced to meet Mom at the door.

"How was your day?" I asked her.

"My goodness! I'm not used to all this interest in my job!" she said, smiling. "But I certainly appreciate your asking. My day was a little better than yesterday, Colm. How was yours?"

I laughed and pretended to punch her on the arm. "Nice try, Mom, I'm Mal."

She frowned. "But isn't that Colm's shirt?"

I looked down. She was right.

"Whoops," I said. "I must have put it on by mistake. I'll go change."

I went into our bedroom and changed into another one of my own shirts, then went back out again. Mom was still by the front door, taking off her high heels like they had thumbtacks inside them.

"Hi, Mom!" I said.

"Hi . . . Colm," she said, obviously guessing.

"That's my name, don't wear it out," I said, wondering how long it would take Tamika to show up. "Did you see Professor Parker at work today?"

She stood up and stretched her back, grimacing like it was sore. "Yes, finally. He was there for a little while in the morning and then again later in the afternoon. Vonetta told me he only teaches one class, so most of his work is research."

"What kind of research?"

"I don't know yet, but his field is anthropology, which is the study of human societies. Even though he was the one who hired me, it seems I'll be spending more time assisting other professors."

Finally, Tamika knocked on the door.

"I wonder who that could be," said Mom.

I opened the door and pretended to be surprised. It was the first time I'd seen her without a book in her hands.

"Hello, Mrs. McShane," she said when I let her in. "My name is Tamika Jackson. I've gotten to know Mal and Colm, and my parents and I were wondering if they could join us at our apartment for dinner."

From the look on Mom's face, you'd think we had just been invited to dinner at the White House. I think Tamika's manners had a lot to do with it.

"Why, it's so nice to meet you, Tamika! Of course they have my permission if they'd like to go." She turned to me with an accusing tone. "You didn't tell me you'd made a new friend, Colm."

"Dinner sounds great," I said. "What time?"

"We'll eat in an hour, but if you want to come down sooner we could play a board game."

That was the perfect touch, I had to admit. Parents hate video games, but they think board games are practically educational.

"We'll be right down," I said.

Tamika left, and Mom went into her room to change out of her work clothes. Now the games would begin.

As soon as she was gone, I went into our room and dropped a Nerf gun on the floor with a loud plastic clatter.

"Hey!" I yelled. "Pick that up!"

"YOU pick it up!" I yelled back at myself.

"MALCOLM!" Mom yelled from her room.

I quieted down for about thirty seconds. Then I jumped from one bed onto the other and crashed down on the floor. I thrashed around, flailing my arms and yelling, "Ow! Stop! Quit it, you jerk!"

"Don't make me come in there, boys," Mom warned through her closed door.

I stomped out of the room, yelled, "I'm going to Tamika's!" and slammed the front door.

Then I tiptoed back to our room, stomped back to the front door again, and yelled, "Well, I'm going, too!"

The door closed behind me just as Mom was saying, "Use your manners! And have a good—"

Out in the hall, I stopped to catch my breath. Whatever she thought was going on, she definitely didn't think Mal was trapped in another dimension.

• • •

Dinner at Tamika's was boring, but in a good way. While we ate pork chops, mashed potatoes, and green salad, Mr. and Mrs. Jackson asked me questions, but Tamika answered half of them for me so I could eat. I said the reason Mal wasn't there was that he was grounded for lying. I wanted to say I was an only child, but Tamika had already told them about the twins she'd met. I could tell they were a little disappointed they didn't get to see both of us.

Even though I still felt bad about the reason Mal was missing, it was kind of nice being on my own at the Jacksons'. They didn't ask any questions about what it was like to be a twin, and I didn't have to compete with Mal. People who didn't know both of us couldn't think of me as the "other" McShane twin.

It didn't seem like a good idea to answer too many questions about Mal, and I knew from stalling Mom that the best way not to answer a question is to ask one so, between delicious bites of pork chop, I interviewed them. I learned that Mr. Jackson was an accountant and amateur jazz musician, Mrs. Jackson was a physical therapist and community activist, and the music playing in the background was a jazz saxophonist named Charlie Parker. Then Mr. Jackson told me about all the great jazz musicians he'd seen until Mrs. Jackson told him that most twelve-year-olds don't find jazz as interesting as he does.

Tamika agreed. "Jazz is boring!"

Mr. Jackson just shook his head and smiled to himself.

I thought jazz sounded kind of random, like an overheard conversation, but I liked her parents, especially her dad, whose jokes were almost as bad as my dad's. Everybody kidded around and teased each other, but nobody got bent out of shape—I think they actually liked being together.

By the end of dinner, I was ready to ask them to adopt me. Unfortunately, Mal and I come as a package, and there was no way Mom would give both of us up.

Tamika wasn't kidding about the board games. We played one before dinner and another one afterward with her parents joining in. I'm not a hundred percent sure, but I think they all teamed up to let me win because I was the guest. Or I could have just been lucky.

I stuck around for a while after that, trying to understand jazz and reading some graphic novels Tamika had lying around. Eventually, Mrs. Jackson yawned and told me they were all going to bed. She was so polite she didn't even tell me it was time to go—but I took the hint.

When I got home, Mom was asleep on the couch in front of the TV, just like I hoped. Her head was leaned back on the armrest and her mouth was open. I watched her for a minute to make sure I saw her chest moving as she breathed in and out.

Without Mal, the apartment gave me the shivers. I got a blanket from Mom's room and put it over her, tucking it in at the shoulders. I wouldn't have minded waking her up for a hug, but that wouldn't have been a smart idea.

I turned off the TV and went to my room, where I made a body shape in Mal's bed with pillows and stuffed animals and then messed up the sheets and blankets on top of it, just in case Mom peeked in before she left for work.

Would I find Mal tomorrow? Reaching inside my pillow, I took out Dad's watch and phone. I wound the watch and listened to its quiet ticking, holding the phone tightly until I fell asleep.

CHAPTER FIFTEEN

THE PHANTOM TOWER

AT TWELVE FORTY-FIVE the next day, I met Tamika at her bench in the Peace Garden. With all the traffic roaring past on Lake Shore Drive, it still wasn't all that peaceful. For the first time ever, I had worn Dad's watch out of the house, because we needed to know exactly how long we had on the thirteenth floor. It was a little loose on my wrist, even though I had tightened the band as far as it would go. The watch was all wound up and so was I.

"Ready?" I asked.

"Ready," she said, closing a book called *Here But Not There: Parallel Dimensions and Other Planes of Existence* by someone named Kingsley van Dash. "I was hoping this book might be helpful, but if you ask me, the author has a screw loose."

We walked back to Brunhild Tower. It looked so solid and ordinary—just brick and stone. But, as I had learned, extraordinary things could be hiding in plain sight.

A taxi van was framed by the tall columns on both sides of the front door, and its driver was helping the Professor get out and balanced on his canes. We waited until the Professor was inside, waited another minute, and then followed.

After Virgilio let us in, Tamika and I watched the 03-04 elevator indicator go up and up until it stopped exactly between the twelfth and fourteenth floors. Then we called the elevator back down and got ready to follow the Professor.

When Tamika saw the *13* button, she gasped. Even though I had told her all about it, I don't think she had really believed it. And for once, she didn't have anything to say.

"Go ahead," I said. "Push it."

She did it quickly, like she expected the button to burn her finger. Then the doors closed and we rode up without saying anything until the doors opened with a *DING!*

"You're sure we can get back out in time?" asked Tamika nervously.

"Pretty sure," I said.

She took a deep breath, and then I took one, too. Locking eyes, we nodded at each other and then stepped into the phantom elevator lobby together.

Right away, I noticed a change in the atmosphere. The pressure dropped so fast, my ears plugged up and my skin prickled with static electricity. The wallpaper seemed to be moving around.

When the elevator doors closed behind us, Tamika looked as scared as I felt. She may not have been my twin, but in a way it was like seeing myself in a mirror.

"Now what?" she asked, her voice sounding muffled.

"I don't know."

The Professor wasn't in the elevator lobby, but neither was Mal. So where was he? I had hoped he would be standing right there, waiting to escape the moment we came back. But maybe he was hiding from the Professor—or someone else.

"I guess we should check these apartments," I decided. "We may as well try 1304 first. Maybe he went in there to try to get home."

Before we could try the door, we heard voices inside. They sounded like the same people Mal and I had heard the first time.

"*Would it kill you to pick up after yourself?*" said an aggravated woman.

"*I think we all know the answer to that!*" shouted a man.

"*For the love of Pete, not you two again,*" said a deeper man's voice. "*Take it outside, will ya?*"

"*You call that outside?*" screeched the woman.

"*Anything to get away from you!*" thundered the first man. "*Where's my hat?*"

As footsteps clomped closer, I backed away.

Tamika tried the handle of 1303. "It's locked!"

I hit the elevator button, and we tumbled inside as the doors slid open.

"Where to?" asked Tamika.

"Let's go back to the lobby," I said. "We'll try again in a minute."

"Who was that?" Tamika panted as the elevator rattled down.

"I don't know, but they don't sound too friendly," I told her. I just wanted to catch my breath and think of a plan before going back. According to Dad's watch, we had about fifty minutes left to find my brother.

The elevator reached the lobby, the doors slid open with a *DING*, and Tamika and I nearly died of fright.

The huge south hallway was jam-packed with men, women, and children. They were playing cards and checkers at card tables, sitting on and in the lobby furniture, even stringing up laundry on long clotheslines that looped from one chandelier to another. Kids were running around like they owned the place, and everyone seemed to be talking at once. The din was so loud, I could hardly think.

It was just like Brunhild Tower, except . . . it wasn't. Everything that was dusty and worn in the real Brunhild Tower was crisp and clean—the whole place looked a hundred years old and practically new at the same time.

"So it's not just a phantom thirteenth floor . . . ," Tamika said slowly.

I finished her sentence. ". . . It's a whole phantom tower."

We looked at each other, and I could feel my eyes growing as wide as Tamika's while the realization sunk in. Then the elevator doors started to close, and I put my hand out to stop them.

"I don't want to go out there," said Tamika in a shaky voice.

"If we go back up, the man from 1304 is going to get in the elevator with us," I told her.

Seeing no other option, we stepped out into the lobby. With all the people milling around—some arguing, some sleeping, some just sitting and staring off into space—it looked like a refugee camp. And things were just as crowded around the corner.

"Where did these people come from?" whispered Tamika.

"They might be wondering the same thing about us," I said as we shuffled into the crowd, trying not to draw attention to ourselves.

The people were dressed like they'd all been invited to an American history costume party, with clothes and haircuts that went from super old-fashioned, to kind of old-fashioned, to not very old-fashioned at all. But that wasn't the spookiest thing—the spookiest thing was how some of them looked almost solid while others hardly seemed to be there at all, halfway between holograms and mist. The more old-fashioned their clothes were, the more transparent they were.

"I'm seeing things," said Tamika.

"I'm seeing them, too," I told her.

"They're not . . . they couldn't be . . . ," stammered Tamika.

"Ghosts?" I suggested.

"But ghosts don't exist!"

"They look like they do. Maybe we should ask them."

The old-fashioned light bulbs in the chandeliers seemed to sizzle. We flattened ourselves against the wall so a blank-eyed lady wearing a bathrobe and curlers in her hair could shuffle past.

"We need to find someplace to hide," said Tamika.

I looked at my watch. We had lost three minutes already. We had forty-seven minutes to find Mal.

"We can't hide. We have to go—"

"Go where?" asked a gum-chewing, yo-yo-twirling boy who suddenly appeared in front of us. He was wearing a button-up shirt, pants that only went to his knees, and a flat cap with a short brim.

"Nowhere," said Tamika quickly.

"That's too bad," said the boy. "I was hoping you'd found somewhere to go. I'm Teddy, by the way. You must be new. How did it happen?"

"How did what happen?" asked Tamika, puzzled.

"How did we . . . die?" I guessed.

Teddy cracked his gum. "I drowned. It was a beautiful spring day, so some friends and I cut school to go to the Cubs game. After it was over, we walked up to

Clarendon Beach to see what was happening there. It was so warm, and so many people were in the water, that we all decided to rent swimming suits."

"Wait a minute," said Tamika with a shudder. "You *rented* swimsuits?"

Teddy shrugged. "What were we supposed to do, swim in our clothes? Anyway, there was a strong wind that day, and I'm not a very good swimmer, so when I got tired, I couldn't make it back to shore. I saw a lifeguard coming toward me in a boat right before I went under. When I woke up, here I was. It took my parents thirty-six years to catch up with me. *They* died of natural causes."

It was hard to pay attention while Teddy talked because I could also see what was going on behind him. He wasn't misty and white like you'd expect a ghost to be—he was in full color—he just wasn't all there.

"Where are your parents now?" asked Tamika.

"They're up in the apartment," said Teddy. "They're terrible snobs and they don't like to mingle, even though we have to share our apartment with four other families. Mom says she doesn't like the fact that just anybody can live here now. So how did you say you died?"

"We didn't say," said Tamika.

"We didn't die, either," I added. "We're still alive."

Teddy's face lit up. "Alive? You don't say!"

Something about him seemed familiar, but I couldn't put my finger on it, in the same way I couldn't put my finger on *him*—it would have gone straight through. I was looking at and through him when I spotted someone even more familiar: the Professor. The old man was heading straight for us with a frown on his face.

"Tamika—look!" I said.

Teddy turned to see what we were looking at. Even though the Professor was still using his canes, he was moving a *lot* faster than he did in the real world.

"That old fellow gives me the creeps," said Teddy with a shudder.

"Is . . . he a ghost, too?" I asked, frozen to the spot.

"He's as alive as we are," said Tamika. Then she yanked my arm and hissed, "*Run, Colm!*"

We ran, weaving in and out of the crowd, dodging the solid-looking people and, with a roller-coaster drop in my stomach, stumbling *through* a wispy little man, as we headed for the stairway at the west end of the hallway. Climbing stairs seemed like a good way to escape a man who walked with two canes, but as we opened the door and looked back, he was moving with mechanical precision, more like a bug or a robot than an elderly man.

"Was it something I said?" called Teddy as the stairwell door slammed shut.

By the time we were at the second floor the Professor was coming up behind us, his breath puffing like a steam engine.

"Wait, children," he said on an exhale. "There's no need to run!"

I sped up. I didn't know how the Professor spent his

time in the Phantom Tower, but I wanted to wait until we got back to Brunhild Tower before I found out.

On the third floor, Tamika yanked the door open, and we rushed into the elevator lobby.

"My apartment!" she panted, pulling that door open, too.

When we got inside, she froze. The apartment was completely changed. The striped wallpaper, the stiff wooden furniture, and the animal-skin rugs on the floor—it looked nothing like the cozy place where I'd had dinner with her family the night before.

She shook her head and snapped out of it. "The back door."

We ran through the dining room, into the kitchen, and out into the service lobby. While we waited for the elevator to come, we heard the thumps of the Professor's canes coming toward us inside the apartment.

The maintenance elevator rattled down, and we yanked the door open and hurried in. Tamika pushed the *B* button while the door swung shut, the elevator starting to move just as the Professor made his way out of the apartment.

"STOP!" he roared, whacking the door with his eagle's-head cane. "I only want to talk to you!"

I didn't believe him, and I don't think Tamika did, either.

Once we reached the basement, Tamika led me down a hall, through a door, and into a huge room where narrow hallways lined with doors stretched as far as I could see. It was practically identical to the maze of storage lockers Mal and I had found in Brunhild Tower.

"There's one for every apartment," she said. "If we find one that's unlocked, we can hide in it."

We went down one long row, turned a corner, and started checking doors. All of them had places where they *could* be locked, but I didn't see a single padlock.

"Take your pick," I told her.

"That's weird," said Tamika. "In Brunhild Tower, people keep valuable things in their lockers, like rugs and paintings."

"But everyone in Brunhild Tower is alive. Maybe when you die, you have to leave all that stuff behind."

"I guess the old saying is true," mused Tamika. "You can't take it with you."

We picked a storage locker at random and went inside, pulling the door closed after us.

We waited in the dark, breathing quietly while we strained our ears for the sound of the Professor in pursuit. It was so quiet I could hear the *tick, tick, tick* of Dad's watch on my wrist.

Just when I thought we'd lost him, I heard a faint rhythm—shuffle-tap, shuffle-tap—his own breath heavy and ragged.

"Children! Children!" he called. "You think you know the secrets of the tower? Well, you'll have years to learn them now!"

And then he was gone.

CHAPTER SIXTEEN

RESCUING MAL

WE WAITED A LITTLE LONGER—to be sure the Professor wasn't coming back—before cautiously opening the door.

My dad's watch said 1:33. Twenty-seven minutes left.

We decided to try the fourteenth floor, thinking Mal might be hiding in the spirit version of our own apartment. But when we knocked on the door of 1404, no one answered—probably because of the racket coming from inside. Tinny music was almost drowned out by stomping feet and shouts of "Aces!" and "Whoops-a-daisy!"

"Do ghosts ever shut up?" asked Tamika.

I opened the door and looked inside. But before I could see what was going on, someone grabbed me and pulled me down the hall into a living room full of whirling bodies. An old hand-cranked record player was amplifying jazz through a giant horn while a dozen ghostly grown-ups danced wildly.

The woman who had grabbed me had short hair, a

fringed dress, and the coldest fingers I'd ever felt. They didn't even really feel like fingers—more like a force I couldn't resist.

"Say, you're cute as a bug's ear," she said, her knees making right angles as she kicked her heels. "Too bad you're a dead hoofer."

A man wearing suspenders and the world's shortest tie twirled his partner, tossed her up in the air, and then jumped over her as she slid under his legs. "Welcome to the wingding, bub. Now shake a tail feather."

My biggest fear in life is dying. My next biggest fear is something even worse: dancing. When I try to move my arms and legs to music, I feel like I'm going to punch myself in the face and fall over. And now I had a bunch of phantoms telling me to dance.

I shook my head, grinned an apology, and started backing up, but another cold hand pushed me back onto the dance floor.

"Nice try, pally," someone said, clearly not ready to let me leave.

Not knowing any of their complicated moves, I shuffled my feet and wiggled my hips while I looked for a way out. Down the hall, Tamika crept closer, trying not to laugh at me.

"He's not a dead hoofer; he's a cement mixer!" said the guy with the suspenders.

"You shred it, wheat!" said another dancer.

Did people ever really talk like that, or was it some kind of special Phantom Tower slang? It looked like the party had been going on for decades: Furniture cushions were scattered, a couple of lamps had fallen over, and the paintings hung crookedly on the wall.

Tamika's amusement at my predicament ended when one of the men pulled her onto the dance floor that had been formed by pushing all the furniture against the walls.

"Come on, doll, ring-a-ding-ding!"

I had to hand it to Tamika: She could dance. She didn't know the moves, either, but after a couple of minutes, she imitated everyone else well enough that they whooped and applauded.

The song came to an end, and someone shouted, "Flip that platter!" I caught Tamika's eye and pointed at my wrist. She nodded, and we both made a break for it.

"Hey, what gives?" said my dance partner.

"We'll be right back!" I lied as we raced into the bedroom and checked the closets.

No Mal.

"Let's try downstairs," said Tamika. "Maybe he was too afraid to go anywhere."

We went down the back way, opening the door without knocking and slipping into a kitchen that looked like something out of a museum: wooden floors, tiny cabinets, and a refrigerator the size of a large suitcase and the most high-tech thing in the room.

A woman in a brown dress was standing there,

smoking a cigarette and looking at her fingernails—she looked so much like a mannequin in a museum that I practically jumped when she started talking.

"And where did you two come from?" she asked, sounding barely interested.

A large man stomped through the butler's pantry into the kitchen. He looked at us and clenched his fists. "Oh, *great*!" he shouted. "Two more. I'm starting to think you're inviting them, Alma!"

Alma rolled her eyes and blew smoke in his face. "I didn't invite them, Orval. I never saw them before in my life!"

From the other room, a weary man's voice called out. "You're starting again, aren't you? For the love of Pete, you two, give it a rest!"

Tamika piped up. "You wouldn't have seen a boy that looks just like him, by any chance?" She pointed at me with her thumb.

Just then, three little kids came screaming through from the other direction. One of them was waving a wooden tomahawk, another aimed a cork-loaded pop-gun, and the third, a little boy wearing only his underwear, had a bucket on his head and was bouncing off the walls like a pinball.

"Who can keep track of anybody in all this chaos?" thundered the big man.

"Look, there are kids all over the place," the woman told us tiredly. "If you want to look around, be my guests."

While Alma and Orval started arguing again, this

time about whether they should sit down for lunch—Orval thought they should, but Alma said there was no point in having lunch when they couldn't eat food, while the man in the other room reminded them they'd been through it a thousand times—Tamika and I left the kitchen. We walked through the butler's pantry into the dining room, which was divided in two by blankets hanging from a clothesline. The man who had yelled into the kitchen must have been on the other side. On the side of the table nearest us, Teddy looked up from a comic book and said, "I see you met my parents."

That's when I realized why Teddy seemed familiar. It wasn't his face; it was his *name*.

"You lived in 1404 when you were alive, didn't you?" I asked.

He grinned. "How did you know?"

"We found your school notebooks," said Tamika, nodding along as she realized it, too. "About eighty years later."

"Has it been that long? I hope you didn't see my report cards," said Teddy. "Look, I admit I could have tried harder."

"Never mind your report cards. Have you seen someone who looks exactly like me?"

Teddy looked puzzled. "Well, if he looks exactly like you, how would I know it wasn't you?"

"He would have been here overnight," said Tamika.

"You are new, aren't you?" said Teddy. "We don't have day and night. It's always in-between."

We had seven minutes left. If we didn't hurry, we were going to get caught in-between, too.

"Can we just look around?" I asked.

"Sure!" said Teddy, dropping the comic book, standing up, and popping a bubble. "I'll give you a tour."

We followed behind, trying to hurry him up as he showed us around. This apartment was a total mess, too, with clothes, toys, and piles of who-knows-what strewn everywhere. Even weirder, every room was divided in half, like the dining room, or quarters and even smaller fractions.

"With so many people sharing the apartment, we hang blankets and sheets so we can get some privacy," Teddy told us, although it didn't seem to be working very well.

The living room was partitioned by clotheslines with clothes drying on them, over which two gangs of kids were having a snowball fight with balled-up socks. Meanwhile, the dance party upstairs made it sound like the ceiling was about to collapse. The room that would have been Mom's bedroom in our apartment was divided into quarters: On a bed in the nearest one, a barefoot old lady snored softly on top of the covers with a wet washcloth over her eyes and forehead. I had a lot of questions for Teddy, but I didn't have time for the answers—he was moving like he had all the time in the world.

Finally, he took us to what would have been the room below Mal's and my bedroom. It was crowded with bunk beds, cots, and mattresses on the floor. In the middle of the room, a big, chubby baby with a saggy diaper stood in a playpen, staring at us while he dug so deep in his nose it looked like he was tickling his brain.

"Don't pick, Hubert," Teddy scolded the baby before turning to us and adding: "Just imagine being a baby forever."

"Mal's not here," said Tamika hopelessly.

"Or maybe he's hiding," I suggested. "Look in the closets!"

I didn't think Mal would have lasted four minutes in this crazy place, but that was about all the time we had left, so Tamika and I raced to the two closet doors.

"He's not in this one," she announced. "At least, if he is, I can't see him. It's full of . . . stuff."

I opened the door of the other closet, and there was Mal, sitting cross-legged on the floor and writing on a folded piece of paper with a stubby old pencil. I was so relieved I almost hugged him—but instead I clenched my fists and got ready to defend myself.

The moment he saw me, Mal practically exploded out of the closet, his arms windmilling.

"WHERE HAVE YOU BEEN?" he demanded.

I backpedaled, blocking his arms and, because I felt guilty, not taking the perfectly wide-open shot at his stomach. "I couldn't help it! We had to wait twenty-three hours before we could come back in for you."

"You have a twin?" asked Teddy, astonished.

Suddenly, I felt a sharp pain, and my left arm went dead. Mal must have felt the same thing—he stopped swinging and grabbed his right biceps.

Tamika was standing there with clenched fists. She had given us simultaneous dead arms.

I shook my head in admiration. I didn't know she had it in her.

"Stop fighting!" she scolded us. "We have to get out of here before two o'clock."

"There's no way out," said Mal, panting. "When you're in here, every floor the elevator stops at is still in . . . whatever this place is called."

"I know how to get out," I said. "And I'm calling it the Phantom Tower."

"Don't I get a vote?" demanded Mal.

Teddy walked over to Hubert's playpen and pulled the big baby's finger out of his nose. "Are they like this all the time?" he asked Tamika.

"Pretty much," she told him, hopping from foot to foot nervously.

I checked my watch. "Two minutes—we have to go, *now*. Follow me!"

With the minutehand ticking closer to twelve, we raced out of the apartment and upstairs to the elevator lobby on the fourteenth floor. Teddy trailed behind, looking too sad to snap his gum.

When I'd seen the Professor go into the Phantom Tower, the elevator indicator stopped between twelve and fourteen, meaning it was on the thirteenth floor, the only way to get in. We were about to discover if I was right about how to get out.

I pressed the button to call the elevator.

Tamika turned around suddenly. "Teddy, come with us."

"I wish I could, but it won't work," he said. "There's a reason being dead is the pits. Come back and see me at least?"

"We will," I promised as the elevator arrived with a *DING* and we got on. "Besides, if I'm wrong about this, we're not going anywhere."

"Hurry up!" said Mal.

Dad's watch was already showing two o'clock. Hoping like crazy it was running a few seconds fast, I pressed *13*, and the doors slid closed in front of Teddy's glum face.

"That's it—we just go down from fourteen to thirteen and get out?" asked Tamika. "How do we know we won't end up in the same place we just came from?"

"We don't," I said.

I held my breath while the elevator went down, then exhaled when the doors opened with a muffled *TINK*. I knew we were home even before I saw the pictures of old Chicago on the walls because it didn't feel like a lightning storm was about to hit. The air felt calm and still—even if it was hot and humid like always.

Mal sighed with relief—and then hit me in the biceps so hard the fingers of my right hand went numb. "*That's* for trapping me. And it's just a down payment."

Rubbing my arm, I looked at the elevator control panel. The *13* button had already disappeared.

"None of this makes sense. Why is that the way out?" asked Tamika.

"You can't leave from the thirteenth floor in the Phantom Tower—" I started to say.

"Because there's no thirteenth floor in Brunhild Tower," said Mal, finishing my sentence. "The fourteenth floor *is* the thirteenth floor."

"And the only way to get back is to take the elevator in the Phantom Tower from fourteen to thirteen," said Tamika slowly. "I guess that makes sense."

"None of this makes any sense at all," I said.

"It may not make sense, but it has a kind of logic," said Mal. "Take the time, for example: The thirteenth floor appears at one o'clock. In a twenty-four-hour clock, or in military time, that's the thirteenth hour."

"So the thirteenth floor is the only one that connects to the real world?" asked Tamika as we finally got out of the elevator.

Mal nodded. "Pretty sure. I tried a bunch of the other floors—I think it all comes down to the number thirteen."

"I can't believe you figured out so much of that," I said, almost wanting to compliment him.

"I've had a lot of time to think recently, jerkface," Mal reminded me.

We went into our apartment, relieved to be the only ones in it. Mal grabbed a bag of chips from the butler's pantry and started shoving handfuls into his mouth as we sat down at the dining-room table.

"Why is the Phantom Tower so crowded?" I asked. "Most buildings would be lucky to have one ghost, but they have hundreds."

"Maybe they all lived here, like Teddy," suggested Tamika.

"But he drowned in Lake Michigan," I said. "Usually, ghosts haunt the places where they died."

"Ghosts don't—" Mal started to say, stopping before he got to *exist*.

"You spent a whole day in there, Mal. You saw them, and you heard them—what do you think all those people are?"

Instead of answering, he went into the kitchen and came back with a glass of milk and two bananas. "I don't know," he muttered. "Once I realized I couldn't get out, I spent the rest of the time hiding in that closet. After a while I got too hungry to think."

I cut him some slack. It must be hard when you learn you don't know everything after all.

Tamika went to the window and looked out.

"Guys, look!"

I hurried over. Mal shoved a whole banana in his mouth and joined us.

Far below, Virgilio was helping Professor Parker into a waiting taxi. When the Professor looked angrily up at the building, we all jumped back from the window.

"I'll bet he's on his way to tell Mom," groaned Mal through a mouthful of mush.

Mal may have been brilliant, but sometimes he wasn't very smart.

"I don't think he will," I said. "If he tells her we were snooping around in another dimension, he has to tell her he was, too. What we really need to figure out is why the Professor told Mom we should move in here."

"Well, at least it's over for now," said Tamika. "I think we should all take the Princess's advice from now on and stay home from one to two o'clock."

"Me too," said Mal.

"Come on, you guys," I said. "Why are you both talking like we're never going back?"

CHAPTER SEVENTEEN

THE PHANTOM CLUBHOUSE

THE NEXT DAY was Saturday, and Mom had the day off. I was so relieved at not having to pretend Mal wasn't gone that I was almost glad to have him back—if that makes any sense. Mom was in a better mood than usual, and I could tell she wanted to make the most of her weekend.

"It's time to get to know Chicago!" she said.

We took an express bus downtown to the Chicago River, where she bought us tickets for a tour boat. Different-sized watercraft, even kayaks, bobbed on the river, and the sidewalks and streets alongside it were crowded with people and cars. We glided under bridges, craning our necks while a tour guide told us about the glass-and-steel skyscrapers soaring above. I wondered if they had thirteenth floors.

After the boat tour, we went for a long walk in Millennium Park, where it seemed like there were a million things to do and a million people doing them. I kept trying to ask Mal about the Phantom Tower without Mom hearing, but every time I tried, she either caught up and made us look at something or we got separated by a big bunch of tourists who were just as clueless as we were. After a few tries, I gave up, realizing there wasn't anything we could learn or do about the Phantom Tower until Mom's field trip was over.

I decided I might as well go along with it. We took off our shoes and walked barefoot in a shallow fountain, where huge video sculptures made faces at us. Then Mom took pictures of our reflections in a giant, shiny sculpture everyone called the Bean before we walked across a silvery, snaky bridge to a playground that had towers, slides, and a massive climbing wall.

When I asked to do the climbing wall, Mom smiled and took the money for a thirty-minute session out of her purse. She was in such a good mood, I was tempted to ask for a full hour.

Behind her, Mal shook his head at me.

I hesitated. Even the half hour was expensive. "Oh, that's okay, Mom."

She put the money in my hand and closed my fingers around it.

"Go ahead, Colm," she said. "Have fun. I'm sorry we can't have treats like this more often."

The climbing wall may not have been as tall as a skyscraper, but it felt high enough to me, even without making it all the way to the top. To my right, I could see blue Lake Michigan, with triangular white sails cutting across its surface. To my left, I could see a cliff-like row of buildings, some of them old like Brunhild Tower. My arms were shaking and I couldn't climb any higher, so I pushed off and let the safety rope carry me back to the ground.

Even though Mal had come at me with the Flailing Fists of Fury after we found him, he hadn't said much about what happened while he was in the Phantom Tower. He'd been quieter than usual since then, too. The puzzle of how it all worked must have been taxing that big brain of his—knowing him, he couldn't stand not having all the answers. I was counting on his curiosity to pull him back in.

Hot, sunburned, and tired, we had to walk a mile before we found a place that sold pizza by the slice. Mom told us we had to try Chicago-style deep-dish pizza, which was so thick it seemed like an Italian casserole. It tasted good, but by the time I was done, my stomach felt as hard and round as a watermelon.

We walked by the river for a while, weaving in and out of crowds of people, going slower in the shade to cool off, until finally it was time to go home. We took the train this time. It started underground and then, after a few stops, climbed until it was up in the air and looking down on houses and streets and backyards. Mal and I pressed our noses against the window, trying to ignore the fact that our car smelled like someone had peed in it, watching the buildings and windows scrolling by and imagining how many stories were behind each one.

The train clattered past Wrigley Field, where the Chicago Cubs played, went around a corner, and then pulled into our stop. We climbed down the old wooden stairs and walked the rest of the way home. Chicago was amazing, and my mind reeled with how big it was and how much there was to explore. But even that couldn't compare with the mysteries in our very own building.

On Sunday, Mom rolled up her sleeves to do some cleaning and made Mal and me do it, too. We sorted the left-behind things in the little room off the kitchen into two piles: trash and treasure. The trash—tennis rackets with broken strings, a rusty electric razor with a curly power cord—we carried down to the bins in the loading dock. The treasure—which included things that still worked and some artwork Mom said wasn't to her taste—we loaded into the van to drive it to the Salvation Army.

There was one stack of things that didn't go anywhere, though: I put everything with Teddy's name on it under my bed. I didn't know if he cared about it, but it seemed wrong to throw out the only evidence proving he existed.

• • •

On Friday, Mal and Tamika had thought I was crazy about going back into the Phantom Tower, but by Monday, they admitted they wanted to go back in, too. Like us, Tamika stayed home while her parents worked all day. And with all her friends at camp, she was ready for an adventure of her own.

"Let's face it," I said as we all hung out on the furniture in the downstairs lobby, with Virgilio smiling at us through a window in the vestibule. "Brunhild Tower just isn't as fun as the Phantom Tower."

"You can say that again," agreed Tamika. "I've lived here my whole life, and this is the first time I've ever seen ghosts having a dance party."

"I'm much more interested in learning why it exists and how it all works," said my brother.

Mal had gotten over his urge to tell Mom, and he hadn't taken revenge on me except for that one hard punch. But that didn't mean he wasn't still planning something bigger. I may not have been able to read his mind, but I could see a look in his eye that told me he hadn't forgotten what I did.

Now that we knew how to get in *and* how to get out, there was nothing to stop us from exploring the Phantom Tower. I couldn't wait to leave our dumpy old apartment and go back. For a building full of dead people, it sure was lively.

First, we played a game of hide-and-seek. Not from each other, but from the Professor. We didn't want to risk running into him, so we made sure we got there before he did. Since we lived in the building and he didn't, that part was easy. A couple of minutes before one o'clock, we called the elevator car to our floor and kept it there by holding the door open. Then, when Dad's watch said it was one o'clock, we stepped inside and pressed *13*, making the one-floor trip before the Professor had a chance to come up from the lobby. Once inside the Phantom Tower, we kept our ears open for the sound of his thumping canes.

Walking up to a basement door marked BOILER ROOM: KEEP OUT, I grabbed the doorknob.

"What're they going to do, frown at us?" I said.

"As long as there isn't some kind of demon guardian waiting in there, I don't think you have anything to worry about," said Tamika.

She was joking. I think. But suddenly I couldn't help picturing a demon guardian—huge and fangy with leathery wings and long, curving claws—which made me hesitate.

"Or a phantom janitor," she added.

Mal eyed the doorknob. "It could just be locked."

Fortunately, it wasn't. Even better, there were no demons, janitors, or anyone else inside. Two enormous iron boilers, as big as tanker cars, towered above us.

Mal, of course, was instantly drawn to a nearby snarl of pipes, valves, and handles. I could practically see his mind calculating as he tried to figure out what it was for and how it worked.

"Cool." He drooled.

"Let's make this our clubhouse," I said, eyeing the ladders going up the sides of the boilers.

"What's the point of having a clubhouse you can only use one hour a day?" asked Tamika, poking a coil of oily chain with the toe of her shoe.

"The best clubhouses are secret," I told her. "Can you imagine anything more secret than this?"

"What about a clubhouse that *nobody* knows about, not even the members?" she asked.

"If they can't use their own clubhouse, what's the point?" I said, exasperated.

"All I'm saying is that would be more secret than this," said Tamika with a shrug.

"What would be secret?" asked Teddy, coming out from behind one of the boilers.

Tamika yelped like she'd seen a ghost—which she had, I guess.

"Hi, Teddy," I said. "We were just thinking this place would make a good clubhouse."

Teddy grinned and cracked his gum. "Too late. Already claimed it. Want a peep?"

We did, of course, so we followed him behind the boilers, down a short hall, and through a door with the word ENGINEER painted on it. Inside was a small room with a bed, a sink, and a table with two chairs. There was a calendar from 1930 on the wall open to the month of March.

"You saw how crowded it is in my apartment," said Teddy. "The whole building is like that, except for the basement. I come here to get away."

The engineer's room was a good place to hide out. You could play games on the table, nap on the bed, and even decorate it the way you wanted, although Teddy hadn't done that. It was spotlessly clean—which made me realize I hadn't seen any dirt, dust, or rust in the Phantom Tower. Brunhild Tower had plenty of all three.

"Does the sink work?" asked Mal.

Teddy shook his head. "You don't need to eat or drink when you're dead. Fortunately, you don't have to wash your hands, either!"

As if he didn't believe Teddy, Mal turned the handles on the sink. Nothing came out.

"If it's a clubhouse, where are the other members?" asked Tamika.

"We had a falling-out—some of the fellows my age are quite immature," said Teddy. "Since then, I've been president, vice president, secretary, and membership all in one."

"Maybe we could join your club," suggested Tamika.

"Say, that's a good idea!"

I agreed, but only if my job wasn't secretary.

"What year did you drown?" asked Mal, now turning pages on the unused calendar.

It seemed like a rude question to me, but Teddy flopped down on the bed and answered like he was telling us his birthday. "1933. I was twelve."

Mal did the math and whistled. "So you're really . . . ninety-seven years old."

Teddy folded his arms behind his head and stared at the ceiling. "I guess that's one way of looking at it. I still feel like I'm twelve, though. I'd rather go to a baseball game than smoke a pipe."

"Why aren't you wearing a swimsuit?" asked Tamika.

That cracked Teddy up. "You haven't seen anybody walking around with a cleaver stuck in his skull, have you? In here, we don't look the way we did the moment we died. I think we look the way we remember ourselves—or maybe it's the way we want to be remembered."

"Have you ever seen other living people in here?" I asked.

"Every now and then, someone will push the button for the thirteenth floor—we usually just give 'em a good 'Boo!' and scare 'em right back onto the elevator."

"What about the old guy with the canes you saw chasing us?"

"Say, what is this, twenty questions? He's been coming for I-don't-know-how-long. He usually takes the elevator straight to the top. But sometimes he noses around, measuring things and writing in a notebook." Teddy sat up and crossed his legs. "Now it's my turn. How many World Series have the Cubs won since I died? I bet it's a *lot*."

"Umm . . . one," Tamika told him.

Teddy looked shocked. "That's all?"

"My dad always said they were cursed," said Tamika, "but I guess the curse was reversed."

"We have to go," I said, suddenly aware of the ticking watch on my wrist. It was almost two o'clock. It sure was awkward having a one-hour-a-day club in a one-hour-a-day clubhouse.

"We'll meet up tomorrow, right?" asked Teddy hopefully.

"Yeah," all three of us said in unison, which made him crack a smile.

He still looked a little sad when we headed for the door, but not as sad as he did the last time. I guess now he believed us when we said we'd be back.

◆ ◆ ◆

"So what is the Professor doing?" asked Tamika as we got into the freight elevator behind our apartment in Brunhild Tower. We were going down to the basement to see if the real-life boiler room looked the same as the one in the Phantom Tower.

"It almost sounds like he's doing research," I said as the cage door clattered shut.

"But Mom said his field was anthropology," said Mal. "That's the study of human societies—*living* human societies."

"Well, maybe ghosts have societies, too," said Tamika.

Through the window in the elevator door, floor after floor passed by as if we were standing still and they were rising.

"But no university would pay someone to study ghosts—no university would believe in ghosts," insisted Mal.

"The Professor does, apparently," I said. "Just like you."

Even though he had been surrounded by ghosts and

just spent an hour talking to one, Mal still didn't want to admit he believed in them. I let it go. The poor guy had already had his mind blown so many times I was surprised it wasn't melting and running out his ears.

Reaching the basement, we went down the hall to the boiler room, which had KEEP OUT painted on the door with the exact same letters as the one in the Phantom Tower.

I grabbed the handle and pulled, but it was locked.

CHAPTER EIGHTEEN

A *MINECRAFT* MYSTERY

EVERYTHING WAS DIFFERENT inside the Phantom Tower, but outside, things were starting to feel different, too. Time, for example: Because we could only go in for an hour a day, time felt twisted and stretched like a piece of taffy. That one hour was intense and over too soon, but the other twenty-three got longer and longer until it seemed like they'd never end.

With school starting in a week, we didn't have many more chances to visit the Phantom Tower. We wouldn't be home alone at one in the afternoon on weekdays anymore, and on weekends, Mom would be around. We might never get back to the Phantom Tower again.

On Tuesday morning, Mal stayed inside so he could keep working on *Minecraft* Brunhild Tower while I grabbed a book and went to the Peace Garden with Tamika. The girl could turn pages like a machine, and she didn't even notice when a giant wasp landed on her fingers and took its time before flying off again. I couldn't concentrate like she could.

One sentence wouldn't really push me into the next one, so I had to read it over. It was like trying to start a broken lawn mower: I pulled the cord over and over, but the engine wouldn't start running. Finally, I closed the book and just stared at the water splashing down the rocks into the pool.

Maybe I couldn't read because I had bigger things on my mind. For instance, if Teddy had died and was stuck in a phantom version of the place he'd been living, did that happen to everybody, or was that just something that happened at Brunhild Tower? If it happened everywhere, then Dad was stuck in a version of our old apartment in Dallas. But that building only had four floors, and it didn't have an elevator, so I didn't know how to get in and find him.

And I wouldn't have a chance to even go and look unless Mom decided she hated Chicago so much that she wanted to move back. I still kind of wanted to go back, but wanting Mom to be unhappy made me feel guilty.

It was a relief anyway to know his body wouldn't look like it did after the crash. According to Teddy, he would be the way he remembered himself or wanted to be remembered. It had always bothered me to think of how he must have looked before he was cremated, but at least that was one thing I could stop worrying about.

At twelve thirty, Tamika and I went back to my apartment and made lunch: a sandwich for her and bowls of cereal for Mal and me. Mal hardly looked up from the computer, only lifting his hands from the keyboard to slurp another spoonful of Cheerios.

Minecraft Brunhild Tower was almost done, without any interference from me, even though I hadn't been able to stop myself from sneaking in a couple of times to fill a bunch of the apartments with chickens. He got me back by erasing all my high scores on *Kart Krashers*.

"Time to go," I told him, just before one o'clock.

"Hold on," he said.

"We have to call the elevator before the Professor gets in," said Tamika.

"Seriously, wait a minute," said Mal. "I have to test a theory."

We gathered around his screen. His avatar stood motionless in the lobby of *Minecraft* Brunhild Tower. When the little clock at the top of the screen changed from 12:59 to 1:00, he went over to the elevator shaft and started flying up. He went past floor after floor, each one of them numbered: *10*, *11*, *12* . . . then *13*.

As his avatar hovered, Mal looked at us over his shoulder, beaming like he'd just won another ribbon for perfect attendance.

"So you made a thirteenth floor in *Minecraft*, big deal," I said.

"I didn't build it," Mal said. "I've never even seen this before."

Tamika and I glanced at each other as what he said sank in.

The Phantom Tower even appears in Minecraft.

"This is too freaky," whispered Tamika.

"Wait a minute, Mal—can you go outside?" I asked.

"I think so."

Mal flew out the nearest window and turned around. There, in the little neighborhood he'd built block by block, sat *Minecraft* Brunhild Tower. Taking up the whole parking lot next to it was the *Minecraft* Phantom Tower. It was an exact replica, except for one important thing.

"It's taller!" I practically yelled. "The Phantom Tower is two stories taller!"

Tamika frowned. "One story taller I could understand, because it has a thirteenth floor *and* a fourteenth floor. But two?"

Mal didn't say anything. He tried to fly through a window on the top floor of *Minecraft* Phantom Tower. For some reason, he couldn't get in. Entering through a lower floor, he tried to reach it through the elevator shaft, but that ended at the seventeenth floor. Finally, he tried going up the stairwell, where there were extra flights of stairs. But the door at the top was locked. And when he tried to mine the blocks so he could replace them, he couldn't do it.

"Somehow this is protected," he said, frustrated. "We can't get in."

"Maybe not in *Minecraft*," I said. "Come on, let's go."

• • •

We found Teddy in the clubhouse, lying on the bed with his arms folded across his chest. He was so perfectly still that my heart skipped a beat. Then, slowly, his lips formed a large, pink bubble that got bigger and bigger until it was the size of a grapefruit. When it popped, we jumped. Sucking the deflated bubble back into his mouth, Teddy sat up and grinned at us.

"You looked like you were—" I began.

"Bored," said Tamika, finishing my sentence before I could say *dead* and giving me a look like it was rude to point that out.

Maybe she thought dead people were sensitive about it. But being dead wasn't like having lettuce stuck in your teeth: Nobody knows when they have lettuce in their teeth, but Teddy definitely knew he was dead.

"I was just waiting for you guys to finish eating lunch," said Teddy with a grin.

"Listen, Teddy," I said. "We know there's a floor on the top of this building that you can only reach by the stairs. But the door to it is locked. Do you know how to get in?"

"Well, you could knock, I suppose. But I wouldn't."

"Why not?" asked Mal.

Teddy whistled and shook his head. "That's where the guy who built this whole place lives. He keeps to himself, and everyone's afraid to bother him. I mean, if he built it, he can probably make it go away, too."

Outside the clubhouse, a metal door slammed shut, the sound reverberating in the vast boiler room.

"Does anyone else ever come down here?" I asked.

"Not usually," said Teddy, looking puzzled. "In fact, I can't think of the last time . . ."

A chain rattled. I held my breath.

Shuffle-TAP, shuffle-TAP.

"The Professor!" said Tamika.

"Is there a way out of here?" I asked Teddy.

"Only the way we came in," he said, cracking his gum. "This is a dead end."

There was nowhere to hide in the tiny room. The four of us wouldn't even fit under the bed.

"Quick," I said. "Follow me."

Remembering the ladders that led up the sides of the giant boilers, I sprinted out the door with the others right behind me. We made it down the hall and into the boiler room without seeing the Professor, even though I could hear his sliding feet and tapping canes coming closer.

I grabbed hold of the ladder's iron rungs and climbed hand over hand up the side of the hulking, riveted boiler. At the top, there was a catwalk so workers could inspect valves or something. Moving as quickly and quietly as I could, I crawled forward to make room for Mal, Tamika, and Teddy.

Peering over the edge, I could see the hunchbacked Professor making his way to the far side of the room. When he went into the hall leading to the clubhouse, I turned to Teddy and whispered.

"Quick—go down. This is our chance!"

Teddy whispered back, "There's something I should tell you about that old man."

"Tell us later," said Tamika. "There's no time to explain."

Teddy shrugged and put his foot on the top rung. "All right."

"*Wait*," I breathed.

The Professor was already coming back. We had missed our chance. Now we had to keep quiet until he left again.

But when Teddy took his foot off the ladder and crouched down to hide again, there was a loud *SNAP*. I looked back to see a sheepish grin on his face. Out of habit, he had cracked his bubblegum.

"Sorry," he said.

Below us, the Professor stopped and looked up. We locked eyes as a slow smile spread across his face.

"So," he said. "You *are* here."

I shook my head. "What do you want from us?"

"Just to talk, Colm. Just to talk."

How did he know it was me?

"Come up and get us," said Tamika defiantly. Her determined expression made me extra glad she was with us.

The Professor chuckled and lifted the cane with the face. "I don't think I'll be climbing any ladders today. Just answer a few questions, and you will be free to leave. But remember, the clock is ticking."

There was an old wooden chair near the door to the room. The Professor caned over to it and sat down with a groan and a sigh. Up on the catwalk, we crowded close together, the metal grating pressing into our knees like waffle irons.

"I'll tell Mom," I said, the words sounding kind of lame even as they left my mouth.

"Go ahead," said the Professor. "Do you really expect her to believe this place exists? Do you think she will take your word over mine?"

He had a point. Since the lying episodes, Mom trusted me about as far as she could throw me.

"Well, you're running out of time, too!" I yelled.

"You are expected at home this evening. I am not. I can wait."

"Sounds like he's got you there," said Teddy, his jaw working on his wad of gum. "Your parents are still alive, huh?"

Mal and I looked at each other. It didn't seem like the right time to go into it, so we just nodded.

"If we get stuck in here for the next twenty-three hours, they'll wonder where we are," said Mal.

"Mom will think we've been kidnapped," I added, picturing Mom coming home to an empty apartment with no way to know where we'd gone. She'd fall apart. One time, when she was having one of her crying fits, she told me and Mal, *I don't know what I'd do if I lost you, too.*

"We hate to leave you behind," Tamika told Teddy. "But if we're not there when our parents come home from work, things are going to get ugly."

Teddy's grin disappeared. "Don't worry, we'll have more time together than you could possibly want. Now that you've moved into Brunhild Tower, you can never leave."

CHAPTER NINETEEN

A CHILLING REALIZATION

"WHAT?!?" MAL, TAMIKA, and I gasped in unison.

Below us, the Professor shifted in his chair and looked up at where we were crouched on top of the boiler.

"Don't you get it?" asked Teddy. "People who move into this building stay here forever."

"I thought that was only if they died," I told him.

"While they were living in the building," added Tamika.

"It's a lot worse than that," he said. "If you *ever* live here—for any length of time—you'll *always* live here."

"Well, that's ridiculous," said Mal. "We'll just move out. Brunhild Tower is filled with empty apartments of people who've left."

Teddy blew and popped a small bubble. "I don't know anything about that. All I know is that we're sure running out of room in here."

Nobody said anything. I remembered how I once, for a minute, wished I could live in Brunhild Tower forever. Had I jinxed us?

"Teddy is right," boomed the Professor from below, startling us. "You will be quite unable to leave. And Brunhild Tower's unleased apartments have more to do with its . . . unwholesome reputation."

I looked over the edge to where he was sitting, calmly rubbing the gold beak of his eagle's-head cane with his thumb.

My blood was hot as lava, and I felt ready to explode. "How could you tell my Mom we should move in here when you knew all of this?"

"I need your help resolving the problem your friend has explained," said the Professor quietly. "Come down here and I will explain."

"That seems reasonable," said Mal, inching toward the ladder.

"Wait!" said Teddy. "This is what I was trying to tell you earlier: He visits the man who made this place. What could you possibly do that he can't?"

"Don't go, Mal—it's a trap!" hissed Tamika.

"But don't you want to know?" asked Mal, his urge to understand more powerful than any fear he was feeling.

In the silence, I heard Dad's watch ticking. We only had twelve minutes left. I didn't trust the Professor, and even if Teddy was right and we were all doomed to spend forever in the Phantom Tower, I didn't want to be stuck there for the next twenty-three hours if I could help it.

"Well, I guess eternity gives us plenty of time to

figure this all out," I said. "But right now, we need to get to the elevator, and, Teddy, we need your help."

Teddy chewed his gum slowly. "I'm sorry I had to give you the bad news. Will you still come back before you die?"

"Yes," I told him. "We're coming again tomorrow. But first we need to get back to the elevator."

"Okay," he said. "There may only be one door, but if you're desperate, there are actually three ways out of this room: through the door, the coal chute, and the boiler itself."

"I'd prefer the door, if that's all right," said Tamika.

"Don't worry, there's no fire in the boiler," said Teddy. "The Phantom Tower, as you call it, is always comfortably warm."

"So the coal chute isn't full of coal?" asked Mal.

Teddy shook his head.

The problem with his solutions was that they were all equally close to the Professor. His chair was in the middle of a triangle formed by the door, the coal chute, and the front of the boiler.

"You're running out of time," said the Professor, his low voice echoing in the tall room.

"Well, so are you!" I said back, getting a little less echo.

He scratched his beard like he was digging for a tick. "I'm perfectly happy to spend the night in here—I've done it many times."

Now we had nine minutes left. Mal and Tamika looked panicked as Teddy shrugged helplessly.

"We're going to split up," I said, realizing it was our only choice. "He can't catch us all. Tamika, you head for the door. Mal, you try the coal chute. And I'll . . . Teddy, does the boiler really lead out?"

"It depends on how good you are at climbing," Teddy said. "There are a lot of pipes to get through."

I was good enough, I guessed. And we were out of time.

"Let's go!" I said. "Make your way back to the elevator and get out if you can. We'll meet up back in Brunhild Tower."

Teddy was closest to the ladder, so he went down first, followed by Tamika and Mal. I went last, taking the rungs two at a time and accidentally stepping on Mal's fingers.

"Ow!" he yelled. "I'm going to get you for that!"

"Wait 'til we get home!" I yelled back.

I thought the Professor would be caught off guard by our sudden charge, but he didn't even try to stop us. More precisely, he didn't try to stop three of us. He climbed out of his chair and, leaning on the eagle's-head cane, watched Tamika run past him and out the door. Then, leaning on the facecane, he looked almost bored as Mal scrambled across the room and climbed inside the coal chute.

I didn't even see Teddy leave, only heard the clang as the hatch on the boiler swung shut behind him. I wished he had explained how that particular escape worked—would I have to climb out the chimney at the top of the building?

The Professor moved forward, smiling.

"You just . . . let them go," I said, glancing at the watch on my wrist. Six minutes left.

His fingers tightened on his canes. "I only need one of you to stay here."

"For what?" I asked, looking for a way past him. "I don't understand."

The Professor was backing me all the way up to the ladder, crowding me, cutting off all the escape routes. He stood so close I could smell pipe tobacco, garlic, and fish on his breath and his clothes.

"Twin buildings, twin brothers—one in each to cast my spell," he said, holding both canes in one hand and clamping a powerful hand on my shoulder.

I wriggled and pulled but couldn't get away—the old man was too strong.

Then I heard a door fly open and bang into the wall.

"Professor Parker!" called a commanding voice.

Princess Veronica!

"Leave us, woman," answered the Professor, looking over his shoulder. "This doesn't concern you."

"I should say thees concerns all of us," I heard her say as she drew closer.

As he sighed in exasperation, I felt his grip loosen. It

was now or never. Tearing free, I flew up the ladder, my legs going so fast they practically climbed over my arms.

"Curse your interference!" cried the Professor, swinging around to face the Princess.

Seeing me as I climbed into view, the Princess asked, "Are you Mal or are you Colm?"

"I'm Colm," I told her, seeing the way out. "I think Mal and Tamika got away."

"You should not haff involved the children," the Princess told the Professor angrily as she advanced toward him. "How many more lives vill you ruin?"

"You're one to talk," snarled the Professor.

While they squared off, I took a deep breath, shoved off, and jumped from the top of my boiler to the one closer to the Princess. I practically slid down the ladder and landed with the Princess between me and the Professor. Behind me, the door hung open.

"Run, Colm!" said the Princess, and she didn't have to tell me twice.

Two minutes left.

I ran upstairs, banged through the door, plowed through the crowded lobby, and hit the elevator button.

"What's your hurry, young fellow?" asked a transparent man in a bowler hat and a checkered suit while I waited for the elevator to come down.

"No time to explain," I said as I got back in and pressed *14*.

The elevator took an eternity to climb, and by the

time I got to the fourteenth floor, the second hand was sweeping toward two o'clock. I stepped out and then got back in, half expecting the *13* button to have disappeared.

But it was there, and I slapped it gratefully, holding my breath while the elevator dropped one floor and the doors opened again.

"You made it!" said Tamika, giving me a big hug that I wasn't sure what to do with. I just patted her on the back until she let go, even though I was kind of sad when she did.

"Sorry we left you," said Mal. "When you said it was everyone for himself, we thought you meant it."

"I meant it when I said it," I told him, "but you didn't have to listen to me. Thank god for the Princess."

"Wait—" said Tamika.

"What?" said Mal.

"She came into the Phantom Tower and helped me get away. He wanted to keep me inside so he could cast a spell. We're lucky he didn't know when you were trapped in there, Mal." Mal rolled his eyes at the reference to magic.

"If the Professor is really trying to help people, why is she working against him?" asked Tamika.

"We could ask her, except now *she's* trapped inside."

• • •

That night in bed, I didn't think about the endless stars in cold outer space. I thought about what was outside the Phantom Tower. Was there phantom land around it, and phantom roads? If Dad was still hanging around our place in Dallas, could I reach him? That was crazy, though. If I left the Phantom Tower and set off cross-country, I might never find him.

And I might never make it back, either.

I set and wound his watch carefully, then put it in my pillow, near the top so I could hear its *tick, tick, tick.* While Mal snored steadily on the other side of the room, sounding like a horse with marbles in its nostrils, I took out Dad's phone and flipped it open. I pressed the buttons and imagined the dead screen glowing to life and hearing Dad's voice in my ear.

Hello?

Hi, Dad. It's Colm.

It's good to hear your voice, son.

Dad? Where are you?

I'm with you.

But where *where. Is there someplace we can be together?*

We'll always be together.

Answer the question, Dad!

Colm, I can't hear you very well. I'm losing the connection.

Dad, are you there?

. . .

Dad?

CHAPTER TWENTY

UNLOCKING THE SECRET

"**WELL, I'M NOT** living in that crowded old tower until the end of time," said Tamika as we walked out of the corner store at the back of the block the next day. We were out of cereal, so Mom had left money and a note on the table before she went to work, but Mal and I had just blown it on powdered doughnuts and chocolate milk.

Mal sat down at the metal table on the sidewalk outside the store. "Just so you know, time doesn't end. It goes on and on forever," he said.

Typical Mal: He has to correct you on some little detail, even when you're talking about life and death.

"It's just a figure of speech, smarty pants," said Tamika. "For your information, we've come a long way since Sir Isaac Newton. Twentieth-century philosophers suggest time doesn't even exist except as an idea humans use to measure and compare things."

I ate half a doughnut in one bite and washed it down with chocolate milk. I can't think on an empty stomach.

"You guys can argue all you want," I said between mouthfuls. "The way I see it, we've got one big, practical problem: We don't want to spend our afterlives playing checkers with a bunch of arguing ghosts."

Mal slurped his chocolate milk thoughtfully. "Are there other options for the afterlife? At least we'd get to hang out with Teddy."

"You saw how crowded it is—and it's only going to get worse." Then, when I realized Tamika was watching us eat, I offered her the pack of doughnuts. "Want one?"

"No, thank you. I already enjoyed a nutritious breakfast of fat-free yogurt and whole-wheat toast with honey."

Mal and I grabbed for the last two at the same time, getting powdered sugar all over our fingers. Tamika rolled her eyes.

"The problem is we don't know enough about how the Phantom Tower works," said Tamika.

"The Professor knows," said Mal.

"No way are we asking him. I think he's keeping everyone trapped and I don't trust him with this spell stuff," said Tamika. "What about the Princess? She did save Colm. All we have to do is wait until she comes out."

Mal grimaced. "I don't want to get involved in whatever's going on between the two of them."

Finishing my last doughnut, I drained my chocolate milk, being careful not to slurp.

"Teddy says the guy who built the place lives inside, on the top floor," I said. "Wouldn't he be the one in charge?"

Neither Mal nor Tamika liked that idea.

"What if he's even worse than the Professor?" asked Mal.

"Mal's right," said Tamika. "Who knows what's in that apartment? If we go in, we might never come out."

"So who do we ask, then?"

"Maybe," said Tamika, "we can find out what we need to know without asking anyone."

◆ ◆ ◆

Back in the building, we hung around the lobby until Virgilio left his station at the front desk and went through the meeting room to the little kitchen where the doormen kept their lunches. Tamika had told us he had a sweet tooth and regularly sneaked off for a quick sugar fix. Mal and I followed him while Tamika slipped out to the front desk.

When Virgilio came out of the meeting room, brushing powdered sugar off his uniform jacket, Mal and I were blocking his path.

"So that old guy, Professor Parker," I said. "He comes every day?"

Virgilio was still chewing what must have been a powdered doughnut. He was a man after my own heart. "Not every day," he said, swallowing and looking embarrassed. "But almost."

"How long has he been visiting the building?"

"Many, many years," said Virgilio, wiping his lips with the back of his hand. He stepped to the right so he could go around us and get back to the front desk.

I stepped with him and blocked his way.

"Who does he visit?" asked Mal.

Virgilio smiled and shook his head. "I'm sorry, but I can't reveal private information about residents or guests."

This time, he stepped to his left and Mal went with him.

"Does he ever talk to you about . . . anything?" asked Mal, stalling.

"Weather, I guess," said Virgilio, slipping between us and walking briskly back to the vestibule. "Now, if you'll excuse me, I have to get back to work!"

We followed him to the front desk, where Tamika was standing with her arms folded and trying to look bored. Virgilio started flicking through papers to look busy, even though the place was as quiet as a library. Then Mal, Tamika, and I went back outside, squinting in the hot morning sun.

"He didn't tell us anything," I told her.

"Did you find anything in the guest register?" asked Mal.

Tamika frowned. "The Professor signs in every day with his name and the time. But under 'guest of,' there's no apartment number, just a scribble."

"Well, that doesn't help us," I said.

We sat down in the shade on a low brick wall that ran along the sidewalk. Cars cruised by on Marine Drive while others accelerated up the ramp onto Lake Shore Drive.

"Is that . . . ?" asked Tamika, looking down the block.

Dante, the nighttime doorman, was coming down the sidewalk. I didn't recognize him at first because he wasn't in uniform and was wearing the kind of big sunglasses grandparents put over their regular glasses when they're driving. He wore a guayabera shirt, shorts, black socks, and white trainers that looked like big, puffy marshmallows.

"Uh-huh," I said.

"He's *old*," Mal marveled.

Mal was right. We hadn't realized exactly how old he was the first time we'd met him. As Dante moved slowly closer without showing any sign of recognizing us, he seemed so stiff and brittle that a good wind could have sent him flying like a sheet of newspaper.

"Good morning, Dante," said Tamika cheerfully when he was near enough to hear her.

He kept walking until he was in front of us, then stopped and turned so slowly that I wasn't a hundred percent sure he was moving until I realized he'd changed direction.

"Beautiful day, isn't it?" added Tamika.

Dante looked down at where we were sitting, his eyes completely invisible behind his enormous black sunglasses.

"It's hot," he rasped as if his voice was something he wasn't used to using.

"You must have worked here a long time," Mal surprised me by saying. "Right?"

"Yes," said Dante.

My theory was that he talked as slowly as he moved and just didn't have time to complete longer sentences, but he proved me wrong when he answered Mal's next question, which was, "So you know Professor Parker?"

Dante's lips curled when Mal said the name. "I know

him," he said, a little faster. "I used to see the Professor every afternoon before they put *Virgilio* on days."

From the way he said Virgilio's name, I didn't think they gave each other birthday presents.

"So he's been coming to Brunhild Tower for a long time?" I asked.

"A long time," repeated Dante, tilting his head downward. It looked to me as if he was thinking about sitting down but afraid he might not be able to get up again.

"Who does he visit?" asked Tamika.

"I can't tell you that," said Dante in his dry, scratchy voice.

He turned and resumed his slow shuffle down the sidewalk, adding, almost too softly to hear: "You'll have to ask *her*."

"Ask who?" I said, even though I already knew the answer.

Dante kept going, slowly but steadily. The sun had moved and our shade had turned to bright sunshine by the time he made it around the corner.

◆ ◆ ◆

Up in Tamika's apartment, we used the computer at her neatly organized "study nook" to search for information about Professor Parker. On the University of Chicago's website, we found a page for the department of anthropology that linked to an official biography along with a photo of him as a much-younger man, before his beard turned completely white. He had a lot of college degrees and had published a bunch of books with boring-sounding titles—he was also *emeritus*, a word that made Mal and Tamika race to see who could be the first to tell me it meant "retired."

"But not all the way retired," said Tamika, scanning the screen. "He's still teaching one class that only meets once a week."

Mal wrote down the building and room number of the Professor's office before clicking to another page.

"Look!" I said. "Mom's listed, too."

Under *Staff*, it read: *Eileen McShane, Administrative & Faculty Support*.

It was weird seeing her name like that, without anything to tell you she was also our mom.

"She's on the same floor as Professor Parker," said Mal, writing that down, too.

"Do you know how to get to the University of Chicago?" I asked.

Tamika nodded. "It's in Hyde Park, which is right by Kenwood, where my grandparents live. We go down there at least a couple of times a month. We usually drive, but I know how to take the L, too."

"So do we," said Mal. "Well, sort of."

Tamika pushed her chair back from the computer. "Look, guys, maybe this isn't such a good idea, with your mom working there and everything. What if she sees us?"

"Do either of you have a better idea for finding out more about the Phantom Tower?"

Neither of them said anything.

"So when do we leave?" I asked.

CHAPTER TWENTY-ONE

THE UNIVERSITY OF CHICAGO

WE LEFT TEN MINUTES LATER—after filling a backpack with bottles of water and granola bars and making sure we had enough money to get there and back on the train. We walked to the Sheridan L station and got on the Red Line going south, reversing the trip we'd taken when we came home with Mom. In the Loop, where the train ran underground, we followed Tamika out of the station and up to the street, climbed the stairs to some tracks that ran *over* the street, and got on a Green Line train headed south.

At the Garfield station, we left the train and walked through Washington Park, which was huge and shady and not very crowded. After we crossed Cottage Grove Avenue, we kept going a couple of blocks and then turned right into the heart of the campus, looking for Haskell Hall. Tamika was following a map on her phone and told us to take a shortcut between two buildings. But then we got turned around, even though Tamika wouldn't admit it.

"These buildings look like they're from the Middle Ages," I said while she walked in a circle, trying to figure out where her phone was telling us to go.

"That's obviously impossible," said Mal. "The Middle Ages were over by the fifteenth century, and America's first colony wasn't even founded until the seventeenth. And *their* buildings were all made out of—OW!"

I punched him hard on the arm, using all four knuckles.

"I meant they *look* old, Einstein."

Tamika started going in a new direction. "This way."

The buildings were mostly gray stone, and some of them were tall and skinny with delicate windows and ivy climbing the walls. It looked like a perfect place for Mal. With any luck, he'd finish high school early and leave for college so I could get rid of him. Unfortunately, we still had two more years of grade school to finish first.

Then it hit me.

"You know what the University of Chicago really looks like?" I asked, hurrying to catch up as we came out into a large grassy area between the buildings and almost running Tamika and Mal over when they suddenly stopped.

"Hogwarts," they said in unison.

They were right—that's what I was going to say.

Haskell Hall was three stories high, with green ivy climbing the sides. It looked like the kind of place Dumbledore would have an office. Or Snape.

"Definitely an old-school *style*," I said, flicking Mal on the neck with my finger and then running up the steps before he could get me back.

A student held the door for us with a curious look on his face, but he didn't ask any questions and we didn't volunteer any answers. The campus seemed mostly empty, so I guessed that the University of Chicago school year hadn't started, either.

I half expected a security guard or someone to stop us, but we just walked right in.

"What's the Professor's office number?" asked Tamika.

"313," said Mal.

"Thirteen—that's kind of weird," I said.

"Just a meaningless statistical anomaly," said my brother, and honestly, I was too tired to hit him.

"What's Mom's?"

"304."

I just shook my head as we started up the old marble stairs.

"Now, it goes without saying that we'll need to avoid your mom," said Tamika. "But what do we do if the Professor's actually here?"

"He can't be—he's stuck in the Phantom Tower with the Princess," I told her.

On the third floor, we turned left and went slowly down an empty hallway, looking at the numbers above the doors. We were in front of 304 before we realized it—through the open door, I saw a few desks and Mom looking at her computer screen, which made me jump backward into Mal, who fell into Tamika, the three of us scrambling to avoid a dogpile and somehow managing to not make a sound.

We hustled back the other way.

"Here it is," whispered Tamika.

PROF. PARKER, read a plaque on the door. Beside it, sheets of paper on a small bulletin board listed office hours, information about the class he would be teaching, and a cartoon with a guy walking into a bar and asking, *Why is this joke funny?*

I didn't get it. Anthropologist humor, I guess.

Looking both ways to make sure the hallway was still empty, Tamika knocked softly on the door.

"Just in case," she said.

Nobody answered, so she opened the door. We slipped inside and pulled it shut behind us.

The Professor's office looked like an old library after an earthquake. The walls were lined with shelves of books, but the floor was stacked with teetering piles, too. The desk was practically hidden under layers of paperwork—I didn't even see a computer—and the windowsill was piled so high with books, magazines, and more loose papers they practically blocked the sun.

"Well, this tells us one important thing about the guy," said Tamika. "He's a world-class slob."

Mal and Tamika beelined for the bookshelves while I stepped over a mound of books to a wall where several framed objects surrounded a bulletin board leafy with yellowed and curled pieces of paper.

"*Survey of U.S. Immigration, 1900–1910*," said Tamika, reading one book spine.

"*Customs and Lore of Itinerant Peoples*," said Mal, reading another.

"Looks like he's an anthropologist, all right," said Tamika, moving to another shelf. "Lots of history, too. And . . . wait a minute . . . *magic*?"

Excited, she started pulling out books. "This shelf has nothing but books and journals about magic and the occult!"

"If he's studying people and customs, that probably comes with the territory," said Mal.

"Or, you know, maybe he's a wizard," I retorted. He did happen to mention a spell.

Sometimes smart people have a hard time accepting obvious explanations.

Dusty diplomas, certificates, and plaques hung crookedly on the walls: The Professor collected college degrees the way some people collect movie posters. There was also a yellow, faded newspaper photo that had fallen to the bottom of its small frame. I carefully lifted it off the wall so I could get a closer look.

In the picture, a crowd of people in old-timey clothes stood behind a thick ribbon tied with a bow; in the center, a man with a white streak in his hair held up a long pair of scissors.

The real-estate developer preparing to cut the ribbon, moments before the tragedy occurred, read the caption.

Someone had penciled the date at the top: *March 17, 1930.*

"Hey, guys," I said. "Look at this."

"Look at what?" boomed a low voice as the door swung open. With his canes planted, the Professor filled the doorway from side to side.

My stomach felt like it was full of ice water. The Professor had gotten out after all. Had he used another elevator—or magic?

"Don't you knock?" said Tamika, trying to sound brave but not exactly pulling it off.

"What are you doing in my office?" thundered the Professor, his eyes blazing above his ancient-ivory beard. He may have looked like a broken-down old man, but he sure didn't sound like one. "Tell me now or I'll call security . . . or better yet, I'll go get your mother."

"We're only here to learn more about what's going on," I said, trying to think. "We knocked, but you didn't answer."

"Well, in that case, make yourselves comfortable," he said, as if there were somewhere to sit down.

As an experienced liar, I could tell right away he didn't believe me. We shrank back as the Professor came toward us. All the space seemed to disappear in the crowded, cluttered room. I bumped into a pile of books, which toppled backward, crashing down and sliding across the floor, but the Professor didn't even notice.

"Fools!" he shouted. "The crone cannot help you. Only I can fill the emptiness we face."

As he moved away from the door, though, he created an opening behind him. Mal, floundering like a moose in a swamp, plowed through the stacks of books and papers on one side of the Professor and half jumped, half fell through the door. As the Professor instinctively turned, Tamika slipped behind his back, so close she could have touched him.

Professor Parker backed up, raising his canes to bar the door and keep me inside.

"Well, Colm, it's just you and me again," he said. "Tell me how much you know."

"About what?" I asked, stalling for time and wondering how he always seemed to know it was me.

"*Don't play games with me, boy!*" he snapped. "I hold your fate in my hands. Answer my questions: Are you working for *her*? Has she told you?"

"T-t-told me what?" I stuttered, goose bumps prickling my scalp as I realized there might be mysteries even larger than the existence of the Phantom Tower.

The Professor stared into my eyes like he was trying to decide whether I was telling the truth. I wanted to look away, but I couldn't—it was like staring down a tunnel and the only thing at the other end was a pair of piercing brown eyes under bushy white eyebrows. Was he hypnotizing me? I would have told him everything, but I didn't have anything to tell.

"Told me what?" I whispered.

Suddenly, there was a commotion at the door as Tamika reappeared, leading a puzzled-looking college student by the arm. "Excuse me, Professor, but this student said he has an appointment."

"Actually, I didn't," the guy protested. "You said—"

The Professor turned, surprised, and I pushed off, diving under his eagle's-head cane and between his leg and the door frame before sliding out of reach along the polished floor. The student stared in confusion as I stood up and took off behind Tamika, who was already running down the hallway.

The formerly empty hallway was suddenly full of name-tag-wearing freshmen getting a tour from an older student. They murmured and jumped out of the way as we weaved in and out of the crowd.

"THIEVES! STOP THEM!" bellowed the Professor as he clomped out of his office behind us.

I realized I *was* a thief, because I was still holding the framed newspaper clipping in my hand. It could have been an important clue or a meaningless memento, but I wasn't about to drop it to shatter in the hall. After all, it had my fingerprints on it.

"Stop them! Call security! Call the police . . . tell their mother!" cried the Professor, his voice quickly getting weaker.

Most of the students seemed too surprised to do anything, but two of them weren't: A boy and a girl turned and started running after us, moving fast on their long legs.

Just as we reached the stairs, I heard Mom's voice above the ruckus asking, "What's going on?"

We took the steps four and five at a time, sliding on the landings between each flight. The students were about to grab us when something they heard made them stop.

"Somebody call 911!" called a new voice. "There's something wrong with the Professor!"

Our pursuers turned around, but we kept going downstairs in a blind panic, half running, half jumping, until we found Mal at the bottom. Then, lungs bursting, we sprinted outside, across the grass and around one corner, then another. Finally, we felt far enough away to stop and rest.

"Do you think he's okay?" asked Tamika between gasps for breath.

"I don't know," I panted. "Hopefully it was a false alarm."

"He could have had a heart attack triggered by the stress of the encounter," said Mal. "Or an aneurysm, or a stroke. It's also possible that the timing is merely a coincidence: He could have a preexisting health condition that has nothing to do with us."

I was too freaked out to bother hitting him. How Mal could be scientific and rational at a moment like this was beyond me.

"Well, Mom definitely knows now," I said.

"And if she knows, my parents will soon," groaned Tamika.

"I wouldn't be so sure," said Mal. "If he was going to tell her about us and the Phantom Tower, wouldn't he have done it already?"

"That's different—that's in another dimension. There's no reason he wouldn't tell her we broke into his office."

"Unless he's worried it will lead her to the Phantom Tower somehow," said Tamika hopefully.

I felt shaky and weird but didn't know what to do, so I just started walking back toward Washington Park. They followed.

"Professor Parker wanted Mom to live in Brunhild Tower, but he doesn't want her to know about the Phantom Tower," said Mal, thinking out loud. "But he wanted to keep Colm inside for that so-called spell. If you ask me, it sounds more like he's conducting some creepy experiment."

And we're the guinea pigs, I thought.

• • •

On the train, I showed the newspaper clipping to Mal and Tamika.

"That's interesting," said Tamika. "But not as much as this."

She lifted the back of her shirt and tugged something

out of her pocket. It was a small, antique-looking notebook with a worn and stained leather cover. As she opened it I could see, written in swoopy cursive: *The Afterlife: Field Notes*.

"It was right on top of his desk," said Tamika.

"I can't believe you guys stole those," moaned Mal. "The Professor will definitely notice that. We are going to be in so much trouble."

"We're already cursed for eternity—how much worse can it be?" I snapped.

As the train rattled north, Mal and I crowded in for a closer look at the notebook. The pages were covered with line after line of neat but tiny handwriting. There were a few charts and drawings, and a few things tucked between the pages, but mostly it was just words. From all the different kinds of pencil and ink and the way the handwriting changed, it looked like he had been writing in it for a *long* time—years, maybe decades.

I had a hard time reading the cursive, but one word jumped out on page after page: *tower*.

"He's been writing down what happens when he visits," I said, suddenly excited.

"I'll read it and tell you what I find out," Tamika promised. "Now we'll know what he knows, too!"

CHAPTER TWENTY-TWO

THE GIRL IN THE PICTURE

IT WAS ONE THIRTY by the time we got back to Brunhild Tower.

"Let's go tell Teddy what happened," I suggested. "I'm guessing the Princess is out already. And at least we don't have to worry about running into the Professor in the Phantom Tower today."

"Or maybe ever," added Mal morbidly.

"We'd better make it a quick visit," cautioned Tamika.

In the elevator, the light behind the *13* button was dim and pulsing weakly.

Mal scratched his head. "That's odd. It's never looked like that before."

I pressed the button, and the elevator rose slowly upward. When the doors opened on the Phantom Tower elevator lobby, something else was different, too: The room was flickering and unstable, jumping around like an old film slipping off the sprockets of a projector. Where the walls, ceilings, and floors came together, I could see starlight winking in the gaps.

"Something's wrong," Tamika whispered.

"We'd better see if Teddy's okay," I said, taking a slow step inside.

As soon as I had, I wished I hadn't. A furious vibration came through my shoes, rattling my kneecaps and making my eyeballs jump in their sockets. I staggered as I turned around, the figures of Mal and Tamika nothing more than dark shadows in a bright rectangle.

Help, I thought, because I couldn't speak. It felt like my molecules were being scrambled—another minute and I'd have been a human omelet.

Then hands grabbed my wrists and yanked me back into the elevator, where I collapsed in a quivering heap. When my eyes came into focus, I saw Mal and Tamika looking down at me like scientists studying a blob from outer space.

"What happened?" asked Mal. "You looked like you were made out of Jell-O."

"Jell-O would have been an improvement," I moaned. "I felt like I was breaking up."

Mal looked into the Phantom Tower like a sailor peering into a hurricane and then let the doors slide shut. "Something's definitely wrong."

◆ ◆ ◆

When we returned to the apartment, something was different there, too: Mom was home. We went down the hall into the kitchen, planning to grab a snack, and found her unpacking a grocery bag. Usually she wouldn't have been home for hours. I think our faces told her how surprised we were to see her.

"We had the strangest day at work," she explained. "I don't really know what happened, but apparently someone broke into Professor Parker's office, and while he was chasing them, he collapsed. Everyone was very upset, so they sent us home early."

"Did they catch the people who broke in?" I asked, proud of myself because this was an especially innocent-sounding lie.

Mom shook her head. "No, and that's the really weird part. Someone in the hall told me it was a couple of kids—a boy and a girl."

"They were probably just messing around," I said. "Maybe they live near campus and were just exploring or something."

Mom stacked two paper packages of corn tortillas next to a pound of ground pork. "It's possible."

Mal wasn't saying a word, and I could tell he didn't trust himself to open his mouth—which was good, because I didn't trust him, either.

"Is the Professor okay?" I asked.

"I don't know," said Mom. "I hope so. He's such a nice old man. Some EMTs put him on a gurney and carried him downstairs to an ambulance. He didn't seem able to speak, but his eyes were open, so I think that's a good sign."

"I hope so, too, Mom," said Mal suddenly.

Mom smiled and ran her fingers through his hair. "Anyway, now that my afternoon is unexpectedly free, I thought I'd make tacos. I can't remember the last time I gave you guys a good, home-cooked meal!"

I was so grateful to be home, and feeling so messed up about what happened at the university, that I went right over and hugged her. Look, there's nothing wrong with hugging your mom. Mal did it, too.

"Wow," she said, putting down a can of corn to hug us both back. "Maybe I'll have to make tacos every night."

We let her think it was about the tacos. We couldn't tell her how much we hoped the Professor would be okay—or that he wasn't the nice old man she thought he was.

Later, while pork sizzled, beans simmered, and the smell of heating tortillas filled the hot apartment, Mal and I went to our room and closed the door.

"I hope whatever's happening to the Phantom Tower doesn't hurt Teddy," I said.

"I'm sure he's fine," said Mal. "He's a ghost, so he probably can't feel anything."

"Yeah," I said, even though it sure seemed to me like Teddy had feelings. And if we couldn't get back into the tower, we were going to have to solve its mysteries from outside.

I took the newspaper photo out from under my bed, where I had stashed it after we got home, so we could look at it more carefully.

Even though the picture was of the people, you could

see the entrance of a building behind them—and that building looked exactly like Brunhild Tower, right down to the double columns on both sides of the front door.

Most of the people were wearing long coats over suits and ties and fancy dresses, and all of them wore hats. There was only one kid, a little girl being held in her mother's arms. At the edges of the picture, I could see some people who looked like they might just have wandered by and stopped to watch the ribbon cutting. In the back, there was even a guy in overalls who probably had to sweep up after everyone else was gone.

Turning the frame over, I bent the metal clips that held the backing in place and opened it so I could take the scrap of newspaper out. It was so old and fragile I was afraid it would crumble in my hands.

"In museums, people wear white cotton gloves when handling rare papers and documents," said Mal.

The way he said it made me want to whack him, but he was right, so I went looking for a pair of gloves. The only ones I could find were the yellow rubber gloves Mom wore when she cleaned the bathroom. After pulling them on, I carefully picked up the clipping. On the back, there was part of an article that was probably carried over from the previous page:

> killing both of them instantly. The real-estate developer is survived by his wife, the Princess of Syldavia, and their daughter. The workman,

known only as "Bricklayer John," was said to have contributed to the building's construction.

"Do you think they're talking about the Princess?" I asked.

Mal's eyes unfocused as his internal calculator went to work. "If this thing happened in 1930, even if the princess of Syldavia was only twenty-five years old at the time, she'd be 113 now."

"The Princess is really, really old," I said. "But not *that* old."

"So maybe she's the daughter?" said Mal, his eyes coming back into focus again.

"Malcolm, dinner!" Mom yelled from the other room.

We put the clipping and the frame under my bed and ran to the kitchen, where I had to make up another lie to explain why I was wearing rubber gloves. This one totally backfired, because I definitely *wasn't* planning to clean the bathrooms as a way of saying thank you for the tacos.

• • •

The next day, we met up with Tamika in the Peace Garden as planned. She was wearing her big sunglasses and didn't even look up from the notebook until we sat down next to her.

"How's it going?" I asked.

She pushed the sunglasses up on her head, and I could see dark circles under her bloodshot eyes. "I read until way after bedtime, and then I started reading again before breakfast, and I'm still only a third of the way through," she said.

"What did you learn so far?" asked Mal.

"It starts in 1948. The Professor, whose name is John Junior, by the way, writes about how happy he was to be the first person from his family to go to college. It sounds like he was the first one to even finish high school. Of course, that was more common then than it is now."

"But what does he say about the afterlife and the Phantom Tower?" I asked impatiently.

Tamika sighed, opening the notebook to the title page. "Nothing yet. Mostly it just reads like a diary of his experiences at college."

"So he doesn't even mention it?" I couldn't believe it—I'd thought the notebook would answer all our questions.

"Not really, but there is some interesting stuff. He talks about his dad a lot—*if he were here to see me now*, things like that. It sounds like he really misses him but never even knew him because his dad died in some horrible accident when he was just a baby."

"How did John Senior die?" asked Mal.

"It doesn't say," said Tamika.

Mal looked at me, and I knew what he was thinking: We had something in common with the Professor. If you never even knew your dad, would you miss him less or more? Maybe more, because he would be such a mystery. I tried to imagine the Professor as a kid, but I couldn't quite picture it. In my mind, he looked like a twelve-year-old with two canes and a big white beard.

"I'll keep reading," said Tamika. "I need to get to the part where he discovers the Phantom Tower."

"Why don't you just skip ahead?" I asked, exasperated. "When I'm reading a book, I always turn past the boring scenes to get to the good stuff."

Tamika looked horrified. "I can't do that. Important details could be hiding anywhere."

"Well, we might have figured something out," said Mal.

Before he could hog all the credit, I told Tamika what we found on the back of the newspaper photo.

"So you think the Princess in our building is the daughter of the princess from the article?" she asked.

"Who knows?" I said. "But there's a picture of a ribbon cutting in front of Brunhild Tower, in a newspaper article that says two people were killed in a freak accident. One of the victims was survived by a princess, who has to be dead by now, and her daughter. Do you get to be a princess just because your mom was one?"

"Most royal titles are hereditary," said Mal.

"Well," said Tamika, "unless we've got a princess surplus in our building, I'm guessing we've already met the little girl from the picture."

CHAPTER TWENTY-THREE

THE TRUTH

ON THE SEVENTEENTH FLOOR, the Princess's door opened almost as soon as we knocked.

"I vas goink out," she said. This time, she was dressed all in purple, but she didn't have a hat or a purse, so it didn't look at all like she *vas goink* anywhere.

"We're sorry," said Tamika, who couldn't help being polite. "We can come back later."

The Princess shook her head. "You vill come in."

She led us into the living room, pointed us to the couch, and then, as calmly as if she were giving us napkins for lunch or programs for a play, put a large cat on each of our laps. I was grateful to see that Mal had gotten the long-clawed, black twenty-pounder I'd had last time. Mine was a skinny calico, and Tamika's looked so much like Eric that, for a moment, I thought it *was* Eric, even though I knew he was probably still snoozing in the sunbeam where I'd last seen him.

Being careful not to disturb my cat, I held out the framed clipping to the Princess.

Her eyes narrowed. "Und vair did you find thees?"

"Do you recognize it?" asked Tamika.

The Princess plucked it out of my hands and held it close to her face, then moved it farther away like she was bringing it into focus. She nodded and set it down on top of the piano, out of my reach.

"Vud you like some tea?" she asked.

"No, thank you," we said in unison.

"You are quite right," said the Princess. "Thees requires coffee."

Ten minutes later, we had tiny cups of what looked like steaming hot motor oil on the table in front of us, and the cats looked like they were daring each other to go for the cream.

Settling regally in her throne-like chair, the Princess stirred cream and sugar into her coffee, gave a loud slurp, and covered her mouth to hide a burp.

Then she asked: "How much do you know?"

"We know that once you move into Brunhild Tower, you can never leave," I said. "And we know that it has a twin you can enter through the thirteenth floor, and everyone who ever lived here goes there after they die. And we know that Professor Parker visits every day—"

"Almost every day," interrupted Tamika.

"But what we don't know is *why*."

"Or *how*," added Mal. "None of this follows the laws of physics."

"And we don't know *who*," I said. "Was your mom also a princess who lived in this building?"

"Let me tell you a story," said the Princess, setting down her coffee cup and picking up a flat-faced, floppy-eared cat by the scruff of its neck. "You haff heard of the Roarink Twenties? Een that time, there vas a man named Vincent Krayfish, who—"

Tamika giggled. The Princess stopped and glared at her.

"I'm sorry, Princess," said Tamika. "It's an unusual name. Please continue."

"Thees Krayfish—" resumed the Princess, only this time I giggled.

"Sorry," I told her.

The Princess started stroking the cat's face, making the fur on its cheeks slide back and forth. "You are both quite rude. *Krayfish* vas vot they call today a real-estate developer. He built glamorous apartment buildinks for rich people to live een. Unfortunately, he built them vith money lent to him by gangsters, und they expected a share of his profits."

"Did he build Brunhild Tower?" I asked.

"You are the kind of detestable person who turns to the end of the book before you haff finished readink," she told me as she lifted her coffee cup to her lips. "Krayfish vas a spendthrift: No sooner had he earned his money than eet vas gone. But the economy vas boomink, so venever he needed money, he borrowed more, built a new buildink, and lived the high life vile the rent money poured een."

I realized the calico in my lap was shedding: I lifted my hand, and the air was filled with lazily floating cat hairs: ginger, white, and black. Feeling a tickle in my nose, I sneezed, scattering them like dandelion seeds.

"*Gesundheit*," said the Princess.

"Bless you," said Tamika.

"Stop interrupting, Colm," said Mal.

"Een 1926, Vincent Krayfish met Princess Vivian Elvira von Andelblat of the House of Hupburg, from a country called Syldavia that no longer exists. Princess Vivian vas touring America under the vatchful eye of her governess. Changing trains een Chicago, she stayed the night at the Drake Hotel, vair, een the dining room, she met the sweet-talking Mr. Krayfish und fell prey to his charms. She did not return to Syldavia. Instead, she married Mr. Krayfish und remained een Chicago. The following year, they had a daughter: me."

"So we were right," I said, giving the calico a polite shove as it stood up to sniff the cream. "But why isn't your last name Krayfish?"

The Princess's eyes flashed. "Because that name, een addition to provoking giggles from children, has been dishonored for reasons that shall become clear. Now let me continue."

"Sorry," I said.

"I am told my father doted on me ven he vas home, but that vas not often. He preferred business und parties. However, ven the stock market crashed on Tuesday, October 29, 1929, he knew vithin days he vud be ruined. His vealthy customers who had been demanding ever-grander apartments suddenly had no money to spend.

Und yet the criminals vith their hands een his pockets ver greedier than ever."

Mal's eyes were watering. I thought he was literally being bored to tears until I realized the big black cat was digging its claws into his legs below his shorts.

The Princess was too caught up in her story to notice. "Krayfish, my father, had only one project under construction: Brunhild Towers. There ver to be two towers, north und south, both of them identical twins. The south tower vas nearink completion, but ground had not yet been broken on the north tower. My father vas een a difficult position: Even ven the buildink vas finished, he vud not be able to repay his loan to the gangsters who had provided financink."

"This is really interesting," said Tamika impatiently, "but I don't see how it has anything to do with the Phantom Tower."

"You children today vant everything *now, now, now!*" scolded the Princess. "Eet should be those standink at the brink of eternity, such as myself, who are impatient. Now hush."

Tamika hushed.

"Krayfish canceled construction of the north tower," continued the Princess. "For publicity's sake, he told the newspapers our family vud be the south tower's first tenants. Then two men varink pin-striped suits took him for a ride een a limousine und explained vot they vud do eef he could not repay the money he owed. Ven he got out of the car, a shock of vite striped his glossy black hair."

The Princess stood up suddenly. Startled, the cat on her lap jumped onto the coffee table, one paw splashing in the creamer, and then scrambled to the floor, where it began furiously licking its paw. Other cats appeared from under the furniture and began circling the coffee table like sharks smelling blood in the water.

Grabbing the framed photo from the top of the piano, the Princess thrust it under our noses. As I had seen before, the man about to cut the ceremonial ribbon had a white streak in his hair like a lopsided skunk.

"You see? March 15, 1930. My father gave a speech, cut the ribbon, und then made his vay to the roof, vair he looked down at the small crowd that had gathered to see the buildink open. Among them vas a young immigrant who had helped build Brunhild Tower. He vas known as Bricklayer John."

The Princess was a good storyteller. I could practically see her father, a cold spring wind whipping his hair and making his nose run as he stood hopelessly on the roof. I pictured old-fashioned black cars scooting up and down the road as waves ruffled the surface of Lake Michigan in the distance. I knew what was going to happen next.

"Vantink to end his troubles forever, my father threw himself from the top of the buildink—but, selfish to his final breath, he gave no thought to vair he vud fall. He landed squarely on top of Bricklayer John und both men died instantly."

Tamika gasped, which made Mal jump and then yelp in pain as the cat dug deeper into his legs.

One of the cats on the floor took its chance and jumped up on the coffee table to start slurping spilled cream. Her mind far away, the Princess didn't pay it any attention, which gave another cat courage to jump up, too.

"Do you believe een magic?" whispered the Princess.

I nodded my head up and down, Mal wagged his from side to side, and Tamika settled on kind of a diagonal motion.

As if in a trance, the Princess felt her way to her chair and practically fell into it. "Bricklayer John's grandmother vas a voman vith much knowledge of this life, the afterlife, und the vorlds een between. Een other vords, she vas a vitch. Ven she heard vot had happened, she placed a curse on the tower: Those who moved een vud never be allowed to leave. She hoped to hurt my mother und me as revenge for her own family's pain. But magic ees powerful und difficult to control. Vot the vitch did not know vas that Bricklayer John had just been hired on to the maintenance staff und moved into a small apartment by the loadink dock. Trapped between thees vorld und the next, thees industrious man vas faced vith the horror of having nothink to do for all eternity. So, vorkink from memory, he busied himself by constructink the north tower een the spirit vorld. He und my father became its first residents. Ven my mother died, after spendink her whole life een Brunhild Tower—vell, she vasn't very pleased to see my father again."

"So your mom, dad, and Bricklayer John are all in the Phantom Tower?" I asked.

Tired from telling her story, the Princess simply nodded.

"Have you ever gone inside it to see your parents?"

"Never to see my father. I tried for years to discover the secrets of Brunhild Tower's curse so I could free my mother und myself—alas, I failed."

"There's something I don't understand," said Mal. "Why is the portal to the Phantom Tower only open on the thirteenth floor during the thirteenth hour?"

"Because that ees the hour the curse vas cast," said the Princess.

Suddenly, Tamika shrieked, and we all stared at her. "I realized something when you said the name John," she said. "The Professor is John Junior . . . the son of Bricklayer John!"

While we wrapped our heads around that, the Princess finished her story in a rush of words. When Bricklayer John died, his young wife had been pregnant with their first child. But because Vincent Krayfish would only hire unmarried men—he believed they worked harder—Bricklayer John had pretended to be single when he moved into Brunhild Tower, leaving his wife at home with his grandma, the witch. John Junior grew up poor but free of the curse. His mom used insurance money from the bricklayers' union to enroll him in a private school, where he eventually won a scholarship to the University of Chicago. As a sociologist, he studied the waves of immigration that had brought his own family to Chicago.

In secret, however, he studied the magical teachings of his great-grandmother. And when he discovered the portal to the Phantom Tower, he had what he'd dreamed of his whole life: the chance to see his father again.

"But he never stopped vorkink to learn the tower's secrets," said the Princess. "I suspect he now knows how to undo his great-grandmother's spell."

Mal, Tamika, and I exchanged glances.

"He told us he needed twins to cast a spell, but he didn't exactly come out and say he was going to reverse the curse," said Mal.

"I don't trust him," declared Tamika.

"But why wouldn't he?" I asked. "He could free the spirits of everyone who has ever lived, or will live, in this building—you, us, everyone."

The Princess used a napkin to wipe cream off a cat's soggy paws. "I think eet should be quite obvious, even to someone so young as you: Eef he lifts the curse, he von't be able to visit the Phantom Tower anymore. Und he vill never see his father again."

Mal's eyes met mine, and I wondered if he had caught the thought that popped out of my skull as I heard the Princess's words: The Professor had no reason to help us.

With a longing look at the creamer, the cat pulled free and jumped to the floor. "No, he ees vorkink on something else entirely," continued the Princess. "Und that is vy he needs you two boys."

CHAPTER TWENTY-FOUR

THE PROFESSOR'S ANSWER

"**I DON'T THINK** the Professor will be able to visit his father today," I told the Princess. "The Phantom Tower seems like it's breaking up. I tried to go inside yesterday, and it felt like I was coming apart."

It seemed as if the Princess only half heard me. Having noticed the feline feeding frenzy on her coffee table, she was scolding them and shooing them off in a flurry of flying fur and splashing cream and coffee.

"It happened right after we got back from the University of Chicago," added Mal.

"It's all our fault," confessed Tamika. "We went snooping around his office and he got really upset and . . . something went wrong. I hope he's okay."

That got the Princess's attention. "Vot do you mean, 'Somethink vent wrong'?"

For some reason, I knew we needed to tell her the truth.

"He was chasing us," I told her, "and then he collapsed. They took him away in an ambulance."

The Princess thought for a moment before answering. "Then our situation ees even vorse," she said darkly. "Back ven he shared information vith me een the hope I had the secrets he vanted, Professor Parker vonce told me that ven the last living descendant of the curse maker dies, the Phantom Tower vill disappear. Any living people eenside at that moment vill be lost forever."

"That doesn't sound so bad," said Mal. "All we have to do is make sure we're not inside when the old man passes away."

The Princess shook her head. "He also told me he believes Brunhild Tower vill disappear, too. The magic bindink the buildinks together ees so strong that the void created by the Phantom Tower's absence vill swallow us whole."

That was bad.

"Maybe he's wrong?" I suggested. "After all, the Phantom Tower may be breaking up, but everything seems fine here."

"It vud be dangerous to assume he ees wrong. Every other think he told me about the towers has been proved correct."

Nobody said anything while what she had said sunk in. I could live with the idea of a boring afterlife—but immediate annihilation? No way.

"We have to go see him and get him to lift the curse," I said. "Who knows how long he's got left?"

"He's going to call the cops as soon as we walk in," said Tamika.

"Not if the Princess is with us," reasoned Mal. "You'll come, won't you, Princess?"

The Princess shook her head and started piling cups and saucers on a tray. "That man vill not help us. There vas a time, perhaps, ven he was more reasonable . . . I knew him then. But the time he has spent between vorlds has changed him."

"We have to try," pleaded Tamika. "You don't want to just go *poof*, do you?"

"I am near the end of my life. I haff little to fear und less to look forward to."

"What about us?" said Mal. "We have our whole lives ahead of us."

"Perhaps eet ees better you do not spend your whole life trapped, as I have," she said, hurrying into the kitchen with the tray rattling like an earthquake.

"What about your cats?" I called after her. "What will happen to them?"

There was a crash as she set the tray down, then silence. Mal, Tamika, and I looked at each other. Maybe we were finally getting through.

After a moment, the Princess shuffled slowly to the door with a softer look in her eyes.

"Will your cats disappear, too, or will they be left alone with nobody to take care of them?" asked Tamika.

The Princess's eyes glistened as she gazed around the room at her cats. Her lip trembled, all her fearsome sternness gone. Finally, she said, "My babies. For them, yes—I vill try."

I had no idea if the Princess would really be able

to help, but I still felt like cheering. At least we had one adult on our side—even if she was a crazy cat lady who was ninety-one years old.

* * *

By the time we got downstairs, Dante was waiting behind the wheel of a banana-yellow Cadillac with sharp tail fins and white leather seats. Virgilio held the front passenger door open for the Princess and we slid into the back seat. It was smooth and cool and, instead of cup holders and a video screen, there were ashtrays and cigarette lighters. The car was in perfect condition, like it had just been driven off the lot.

"One thing I don't get about the Phantom Tow—" I started to say, gasping when Mal jabbed me just under the ribs.

"Shh!" he hissed, pointing through the seat back at Dante.

"You may say the same thinks to him as you vud to me," said the Princess. "My old und loyal friend Dante shares our fate. You see, as a young man, he moved into the apartment by the loadink dock that vas briefly Bricklayer John's home."

Dante drove the same way he walked: slow as a glacier. Before pulling into traffic, before even turning his head to look for oncoming cars, he let the turn signal click for a good thirty seconds. And when he stepped on the gas, it was like he barely had the strength to push down. Once we were on Lake Shore Drive, he crawled along in the right-hand lane while the other cars roared past us like they were in the Indy 500.

"There's something I still don't understand," I said. "If we can leave whenever we want, how are we trapped? Shouldn't the curse keep us in the building?"

"Eets enchantment ees much more insidious than that," said the Princess over her shoulder. "After all, do you not go to the park? Does your mother not leave for vork? But! Eef you try to move away, thinks begin to go wrong. Your car vill not start. The job you are promised ees suddenly not available. Your new house burns down. Und, through some combination of circumstances, you find yourself back at Brunhild Tower."

Tamika looked up from the notebook like she had been listening all along. "And there's something I don't understand, either: If you were born and raised in Chicago, why do you talk like you're from Syldavia, a country that doesn't even exist anymore?"

For a moment, the Princess didn't move or speak. Cars zoomed by so fast it felt like we were standing still. Mal raised his right eyebrow at me, and I raised my left one at him.

Now she's done it, I thought at him, and he nodded.

Had we finally achieved twin telepathy?

"I know what you're thinking," he whispered. "You wish you'd asked that question."

I sighed.

The Princess sighed, too.

"You're a smart girl, Tamika," said the Princess, her accent suddenly gone. "This is what I sound like when I talk to my cats. But my whole life, when I've been in public, I've talked just like my mother."

You could have knocked me over with a paper clip. She sounded totally normal, like someone you'd meet at the grocery store.

"But why?" asked Tamika.

"If you could choose between being an old lady who watches too much TV and reads too many gossip magazines or a mysterious princess from a foreign land, which one would you rather be?"

"A princess, obviously," said Tamika.

"Und how vud the Princess of Syldavia sound?" asked the Princess.

"I get it," said Tamika, and I did, too, although Mal looked like he was still running the code and checking for errors.

"You can talk however you want around us," I said. "You're still a princess. And as far as I'm concerned, you're very mysterious."

"Thank you, Colm," said the Princess in her Chicago voice. "That's really nice of you."

◆ ◆ ◆

Dante didn't drive fast, but at least he got us to the University of Chicago Medical Center in Hyde Park without getting rear-ended by an express bus. The blue summer sky was turning dark with clouds as he dropped us off at the entrance and went to park the car. Closing the notebook, Tamika told us she'd gotten to a part where the Professor had begun to research his family history.

"Not helpful," said my brother.

"Well, I'm sorry, Mal," said Tamika, "but I can't make up stuff that isn't there."

We followed the Princess into the hospital. She went into full royalty mode at the front desk, and I could see why. When she introduced herself as Princess Veronica Margareta von Andelblat in her old-school accent, the receptionists acted like she was in charge instead of them.

I wondered if I would be able to get away with a cool accent when school started, maybe an Irish accent like Dad and Grandma and Grandpa McShane—after all, nobody knew me in Chicago. It would only work if Mal did it, too, though. And only if we didn't get vaporized first.

Finally, in the intensive care unit, we found the right room, where a sliding glass door was open, but a curtain covered the doorway. *Parker* was written in marker on a little dry-erase board. Pulling the curtain to one side, we went in.

◆ ◆ ◆

The Professor was in bed with his white beard resting on top of his hospital gown and an IV tube in his arm. Beside him, a heart monitor beeped softly. The old man looked so weak and deflated that I wanted to turn around and leave. If we were responsible for what had happened to him, I didn't want to be there when he woke up.

I could see hate in the Princess's eyes but also fear—she was nervous, too. Then, straightening her shoulders, she went to his side and put her hand on his arm.

"Professor Parker," she said crisply in her princess voice.

He didn't answer, so she said it louder, gently moving his arm.

Still snoozing, the Professor smacked his lips and groaned, like he was having a disappointing dream about food.

"Professor Parker!" barked the Princess, shaking his arm like a rag doll.

The Professor sat straight up with his eyes wide and shouted, "I'LL HAVE YOU ALL HANGED!"

Everyone jumped back. Mal bumped into a bedside table and sent it rolling across the floor.

I guess the Professor's dream was about the Wild West, not food. As he woke up, his eyes slowly focused as he took us all in.

"I see I was right," he croaked. "You've been working for the old lady all along."

"We weren't working for anybody," I said.

The Professor lay back on his pillow, like he was already running out of energy.

"Then for whom were you spying when you broke into my office and nearly killed me?"

"We're very sorry about that," said Tamika.

"I can see you're sorry for nothing," said the Professor, his eyes glittering. "You are thieves, and if you had any conscience at all, you would return what you have taken."

"We left it at home," I lied, hoping he didn't have X-ray vision and could see his notebook in Tamika's pocket.

"You haff a lot of nerve speakink to them like that," said the Princess coldly. "Eef you had lifted the curse ven you first learned how to do eet, eef you ver not keeping so many souls imprisoned for your own selfish ends, you vud not haff children sneakink into your office searchink for answers."

"Breaking and entering—" sputtered the Professor.

"It *was* unlocked," Mal reminded him.

"*Stealing*, and giving an old man a heart attack. How dare you make these accusations to a dying man," he roared, or tried to, as his voice was lost in a hacking cough.

The heart monitor was beeping more quickly, the peaks and valleys on its screen getting closer and closer together.

The Princess sat down in a chair by the bed and looked into his eyes.

"Maybe you are dyink und maybe you aren't," she said. "But you vill soon—und I vill, too. Und before ve go, you must lift the curse. You do know how, don't you?"

Looking defiant, he nodded in confirmation.

"Then eet ees time to do vot ees right," said the Princess.

"You call it a curse," said the Professor, pressing a button to raise his bed. "To me, it has been quite the opposite—a gift! If it were not for my great-grandmother's spellcraft, I would never have known my father. You can't imagine how alone in the world I felt until we were reunited."

"Ees that truly your father?" asked the Princess. "A spirit preserved for all eternity at the same age as his last day on earth?"

The Professor opened his mouth and then closed it without answering. His shaggy white head sank back into the pillow.

"You are foolish as vell as stubborn," continued the Princess. "Eef you die vithout liftink the curse, you vill not join him. After all, you haff never lived een Brunhild Tower."

"And even if you *do* move in, the whole thing ends when you do," added Mal, with his usual sensitivity.

The Professor spoke in a weary monotone. "You know much but understand little. Yes, if I simply moved in to Brunhild Tower, the Phantom Tower, as you call it, would still vanish with my death. But my life's work was not to lift the curse—I planned to extend it forever, so it would go on even after my death in this world. Only then would I move into the tower. Only then would I be with my father for all eternity."

The room was quiet, except for the beep of the heart monitor, which was slowing down again. I thought about my own fraying connection with Dad and wondered just how far I would go to keep it from breaking entirely. The Professor was so still, it was like he'd forgotten we were there.

"So why did you drag us into this?" I asked. "Why did you tell Mom it was such a great idea to move in?"

"All I needed was a pair of twins, one in each tower while I spoke the words to strengthen the curse. When your mother mentioned you during her interview, I knew the final piece had fallen in place." He pointed at the Princess. "Had this infernal woman not intervened before I trapped you inside, I could have cast the spell. But I failed, and I am damned either way."

"Then set the rest of us free und LIFT THE CURSE!" cried the Princess.

Lifting himself up on his elbows and coughing to clear his throat, the Professor stared coldly at her.

"Your father took my father away from me once," he said. "If I lose him again, it will not be for you or anyone else. My answer is no."

CHAPTER TWENTY-FIVE

DOOMED

"WHAT WILL BECOME of my poor little kitties?" the Princess wailed from the front seat as Dante drove home so slowly that I was tempted to get out and walk. After the Professor's defiant answer, the Princess had ordered him to help, and then begged him, but neither approach worked.

Fat raindrops began to hit the windshield like juicy bugs: *splat, splat, splat.*

What will become of Teddy? I thought. *And all of us?* A tiny part of me sympathized with the Professor, but he was so selfish, it was like he didn't care if the world burned down as long as he had a cool place to sit.

"I knew that man vud not help us! I told you!" she said, switching in and out of her Syldavian accent. She must have been too upset to keep track of how she sounded.

"Listen," I told Mal and Tamika over the Princess's babbling. "We're going to have to lift the curse with or without the adults' help. The Professor said he knows the secret, so it must be in that notebook."

Tamika had *Field Notes* open in her lap, but I hadn't seen her turn a page since we'd left the hospital. I was starting to think she read as slowly as Dante drove.

Mal was watching her, too, his fingers twitching like he was going to reach out and do it for her.

"Come on, Tamika, read faster!" asked Mal.

"I told you: If I skim, I might miss something important," said Tamika defensively.

"Maybe we can help," I suggested. "We could tear pages out of the notebook. If all three of us are looking, we should find the answer more quickly."

Tamika handed me the notebook. "Be my guest."

While cars roared by on both sides, I opened the notebook to where the pages were marked with a ribbon and started reading—that is, I *tried* to, but the Professor's handwriting looked like a doctor writing backward. I could pick out *a*, *and*, and *the*, and the word *tower* still jumped out, but everything else was gobbledygook.

"How can you read this, Tamika?" I asked.

"Like I said: slowly. His penmanship gets worse every year."

I gave the notebook back. "Keep up the good work. Just make sure you find it before the Professor dies and we're all obliterated."

"No pressure, Tamika," said Mal.

"Thanks *a lot*," she said.

◆ ◆ ◆

It was pouring rain when Dante finally dropped us off at Brunhild Tower. Virgilio came out with an umbrella to keep us from getting soaked. The Princess went home to check on her cats while we went up to our apartment. Tamika sat down on our couch and Eric curled up on top of her while Mal got on the computer and explored *Minecraft* Brunhild Tower, looking for clues. I don't know what he expected to find, but I guess it was better than doing nothing.

"I can't believe we were part of the Professor's plan all along," I said. "We wouldn't even have moved to Chicago if he hadn't offered her a job."

"I guess it's no stranger than everything else," said Mal, tapping on his keyboard.

"Doesn't it make you mad?" I asked.

"I want to believe I wouldn't have done the same thing if I were in his shoes," he said, still not looking up from the screen. "But I'm not a hundred percent sure that's true. That doesn't mean I don't want to ruin his plans."

At one o'clock, I went to the thirteenth floor to check on the Phantom Tower. It still didn't look normal—if a ghostly apartment building in another dimension *could* look normal—but it didn't seem to be vibrating as much as the day before. Taking a chance, I stepped inside.

My ears plugged, and it felt like I was standing on a paint mixer—but at least my molecules weren't being scrambled. I breathed deeply and let the elevator doors close behind me. Without dad's watch, I couldn't keep track of time, but I wanted to find Teddy and tell him we hadn't forgotten about him.

I turned the handle of 1304, opened the door, and went inside. It was eerily quiet. For once, there were no arguing voices, no screaming kids.

I tiptoed down the hall into the kitchen: no one. I went through the butler's pantry into the dining room and stopped. Teddy's parents, Alma and Orval, were hugging each other—and between them was Teddy.

"What will be will be," murmured Alma. "It's not in our hands now."

Obviously, the people inside the Phantom Tower knew something was wrong, too. They couldn't know the details, but it was clear their home was changing and none of them knew what was next.

I was tempted to interrupt them and tell them what I'd learned, but I realized I didn't have any answers that would help. We still didn't know how to lift the curse, and if the Professor died before we could do it, we were all in the same boat.

I backed up slowly, then made my way out to the entry hall and got ready to leave.

Then I realized it wasn't as quiet as I'd thought. Throughout the apartment, I could hear quiet voices, sniffling, and crying. It was like they were having the funeral in advance.

I also heard someone say, "Aw, go ahead and let Hubert pick his nose. What does it matter now?"

I eased the door open and was about to slip out when a little kid came around the corner and saw me. He was wearing a cowboy vest and an empty holster, and his hair was sticking up in back.

"What's gonna happen?" he asked. "All the grown-ups are scared."

"I don't know," I told him.

I closed the door, ran up the fire stairs to fourteen, and called the elevator. I guess the ghosts had just as many questions as the living—but even less power to change their fates.

• • •

When I got back to the apartment, there was a change in the atmosphere there, too. Mal had joined Tamika on the couch, and the two of them were talking excitedly while they looked at the pages of the Professor's notebook and thunder rumbled outside.

They both looked up when I came into the room.

"We found it!" said Mal.

"Well, I found it," said Tamika. "I was just showing Mal."

With a sudden feeling of hope, I sat down on the other side of Tamika so I could see what they were looking at—but, if anything, the Professor's handwriting had gotten even worse.

"Can you please translate that?" I asked.

"After he discovered the Phantom Tower and was reunited with his father, the Professor did everything he could to find out how to lift the curse. He interviewed old people he thought might know magic, he read old books in forgotten libraries, and eventually, he started traveling to Eastern Europe to seek out more old people and books."

"Did he go to Syldavia?" asked Mal.

Tamika stood up and started pacing while she talked, moving the notebook like a conductor's baton. I had never seen her so excited.

"The Princess's mom is from Syldavia, not the Professor's great-grandma. But by random chance—or maybe it was fate—Bricklayer John was from Rumoria, which was right next door. In an old Rumorian library, in a special collection of uncategorized scrolls, Professor Parker found this curse-breaking spell."

Mal and I were on the edge of our seats as Tamika straightened her back and started to read. As the rain fell even harder, it got so dark it seemed like the sun was going down.

"*To lift the curse of eternal dwelling,*" she began.

"Wait," I interrupted. "If you read it now, will the curse be lifted?"

Tamika shook her head. "It's not as easy as that. You have to gather a bunch of stuff and then say some specific words while you do certain things."

"Okay, so what are the things?"

"*To lift the curse of eternal dwelling*," Tamika began again, "*gather you these things: the blood of the living, the hair of the dead. Gather you also that which they wear in death.*"

My head was spinning. This sounded like real, live magic. "Keep going," I urged her.

"Wait a minute," said Mal. "Slow down. Forget about the rest of the spell until we figure this out."

"It's simple," said Tamika. "The blood of the living must mean the Princess and the Professor, and the hair of the dead would be Vincent Krayfish and Bricklayer John."

"We also need the clothes they were buried in," I added.

Mal groaned. "I'll tell you something else that's simple: We're doomed."

"There's no guarantee this will work, of course," said Tamika as she closed the notebook. "He obviously hasn't tried it. Once he learned how it worked, he realized that what he really wanted was for the curse to last forever."

I hit Mal in the arm with four knuckles. "We're only doomed if we give up. Come on, Mal, *think*," I told him.

"I *think* we're doomed," he said.

Outside, the rain poured down.

CHAPTER TWENTY-SIX

AN UNTIMELY SURPRISE

THE NEXT DAY WAS FRIDAY, the last day before a three-day weekend. Monday was Labor Day, and Mal and I were supposed to start at our new school on Tuesday. Normally, I would have been dreading that, but now I was starting to think if school started as planned on Tuesday, it would be the best thing ever because it would mean the world hadn't come to an end.

In the morning, Mal, Tamika, and I wrote down all the things we needed to reverse the curse—it looked like a creepy stalker's Christmas list.

Mal was right—it did look hopeless. But I was also right, because doing nothing would have *really* been hopeless. None of the things were easy to get, but we had to start somewhere. And with the weekend coming, it was our last chance to go into the Phantom Tower without Mom hanging around.

First, we went to see the Princess, who answered the door wearing a bathrobe and curlers. She had always seemed so proud of her appearance that it was strange to see her all slobbed out. When she saw us, she shrugged, turned around, and went into her apartment, leaving the door open for us to follow.

She lay down on the couch and rested the back of her hand on her forehead. A half-dozen cats who had been lined up on the back of the couch tumbled down on her in a furry avalanche.

"I don't know a polite way to say this," I said, "but we need some of your blood."

I expected her to be surprised or offended, but she just held out her wrist.

"Take as much as you want," she said. "I don't need it anymore."

"Don't give up, Princess," said Tamika. "We found out how to lift the curse."

The old woman lifted her hand from her forehead and grimaced while the cats jockeyed for position on her lap. "I spent my whole life trying, and you found the secret in two weeks? I don't believe it."

Tamika held up the notebook. "You didn't have this."

"I guess I didn't have you, either," said the Princess with a grim smile.

"Go ahead, Mal," I said, stepping aside.

The Princess raised her eyebrows as Mal pulled over a footstool and opened his chemistry kit. After cleaning her finger with an alcohol swab, he used a sterile needle to prick her finger, which made her flinch and say what sounded like a bad word in Syldavian. Then he carefully squeezed a few bright-red drops of blood into a glass test tube.

Tamika, who had written our list on a blank page in the back of the Professor's notebook, put a check mark next to *Blood from the living: the Princess.*

"Now, do you have some of your father's hair?" I asked.

"What do you think this is, a barbershop?" snapped the Princess. "Vy would I have *hair* lying around?"

Actually, with all the cat hair on the floor, it *did* kind of look like a barbershop—if we swept her apartment, we probably would have found enough to make a whole new cat.

"Sometimes people save it as a memento," said Tamika, hoping to jog her memory. "Baby's hair, first haircuts, stuff like that."

The Princess gasped and sat up. All the cats jumped off except the big black one, which hung on to her robe like a bear cub on a tree. The Princess stood and left the room, returning a moment later with a necklace dangling from one hand and the cat still attached to her bathrobe.

She gave the necklace to Tamika. "My mother's locket. I had forgotten all about it."

Tamika opened the small heart-shaped locket. A tuft of jet-black hair was curled inside.

"Frankly, I'm surprised she didn't burn it," said the Princess.

We needed blood from the Professor and hair from Bricklayer John, too, but we had already decided to put those off until last. If we even got to that part, it would be a miracle.

As Tamika put a check mark by *Hair of the dead: Vincent Krayfish*, Mal moved on to our next challenge.

"This is great and everything, but how are we going to get clothes from Krayfish and Bricklayer John? Their bodies are six feet underground."

"Actually, I believe Bricklayer John was cremated," said the Princess.

"Even worse," said Mal.

"Maybe the instructions don't mean what they wore in their coffins," I said. "What if we use something they're wearing in the Phantom Tower?"

"Can their clothes come out even if they can't?" wondered Tamika. "The notebook doesn't say anything about it."

"I have been in and out of the spirit world, but it never occurred to me to bring back someone's dirty laundry," said the Princess.

"Well, if we don't want to become thieves *and* grave robbers, I guess we have to try," I said.

• • •

It was already after noon, so we headed back to our apartment to wait until the thirteenth floor opened. I hoped the Professor was still getting better—if his condition had taken a turn for the worse, we might not be able to navigate the Phantom Tower at all.

When we opened our front door, though, we found a different problem waiting: Mom.

"Surprise!" she said, coming out of the kitchen with

an ear-to-ear smile. "Oh, hello, Tamika. It turns out the department has a tradition of giving everyone the afternoon off on the Friday before Labor Day."

This was terrible. How were we going to lift the curse with Mom hanging around?

"That's awesome, Mom," I said, trying my best to make it sound like it really was. "How's Professor Parker doing?"

Her smile faded. "A little better, I heard. That's very thoughtful of you. When he comes back to work, I'll tell him you asked about him."

It was time to change the subject. "So what are you going to do with your free time? Take a nap? Go shopping?"

"That's the real surprise," she said. "The sun has dried up all the rain, so we're going to have a picnic lunch at the beach. I have plenty of food, and you are more than welcome to join us, Tamika."

We followed Mom into the kitchen and saw that she had bought lunch meat, sliced cheese, grapes, sodas, and my favorite kind of chips. The sight of the chips made my mouth water, but I didn't have time to think about eating.

"She can't come," blurted Mal.

Mom frowned. "Let the young lady speak for herself."

"He's right. I can't," said Tamika slowly, trying to come up with a good explanation after Mal put her on the spot. "I . . . have to . . . do homework. My summer reading project isn't finished."

That wasn't true, of course. Tamika had told us

she finished her summer reading project before school was even out last June. Thankfully, Mom didn't know Tamika very well.

"Are you sure?" asked Mom. "It would be a shame to do homework on a beautiful day like this."

"I'm sure, Mrs. McShane," said Tamika solemnly. Then, with a meaningful look at me and Mal, she added, "I'm usually a fast reader, but this particular text is very dense—and I wouldn't dream of skimming."

"We can't go on a picnic, either, Mom," I said, thinking fast. "We need to do the summer project, too."

Big mistake. Mom didn't believe me for a second, mainly because I had never volunteered to do homework in my life.

Nice one, doofus, Mal would have thought at me if he wasn't too logical to use telepathy.

And you have a better idea? I thought back, knowing he wouldn't answer.

Mom frowned. "No teacher on earth would expect you to do a summer project if you weren't enrolled when it was assigned the previous spring. Now, come on. I have some time off, and we are going to enjoy it as a family."

From the look on her face, I knew there was no way she was going to give in. She wanted us all to have fun together even if it killed us.

Mal was right: We were doomed.

CHAPTER TWENTY-SEVEN

TOTAL CHAOS

I COULD FEEL precious seconds ticking by as Mom finished packing for the trip to Montrose Beach. While she rummaged around looking for sunscreen, beach towels, sunglasses, and sandals, any chance we had of making it into the Phantom Tower was slipping away.

"What are we going to do?" hissed Mal frantically.

We were in our bedroom, changing into our swimsuits as Mom instructed. He was the one with a computer for a brain. Why couldn't he compute a solution for once? The problem was that he could solve any problem—as long as it didn't have real consequences.

"Listen, Mal, just follow along and try not to screw things up."

I slipped Dad's watch into my pocket. Then we pulled on T-shirts and sandals and went back to the kitchen, where Mom was toasting bread for sandwiches. Instead of acting reluctant to go along, I sighed loudly and stamped my foot.

"Be patient, Colm," said Mom, taking the mayonnaise out of the fridge. "I'll be finished soon."

"But I want to go *now*," I whined, even annoying myself. Mal shot me a look.

"But we can't go to the beach," he said under his breath. Honestly, sometimes I couldn't believe his grades were better than mine.

"You could always help make sandwiches," she suggested.

"I have a better idea: You could meet us at the beach. We know how to get there already. We'll be at the lifeguard stand farthest away from the dog beach."

Finally, she gave in. "All right. But take your towels with you. I don't want to carry everything. And be careful crossing that busy intersection!"

We grabbed the towels and headed out the door. I felt bad about lying to her because I knew she'd worry when she couldn't find us at the beach. But as soon as we got the things we needed from the Phantom Tower, we'd hurry over there and act like she'd heard us wrong. How freaked out could she get in an hour?

◆ ◆ ◆

"I thought I was going to have to go in without you," said Tamika impatiently when we met up with her at the Peace Garden. "It's almost one o'clock!"

"Sorry," I told her. "It's impossible to talk Mom out of family time, so we had to just use a big, fat lie."

"This better work," said Mal, "because I have a feeling we're going to be grounded for the rest of our lives."

We went back through the tunnel under Lake Shore Drive and walked up the sidewalk to a hedge a half block from our building, where we could see Mom leave without her seeing us.

I fastened Dad's watch on my wrist as the minute hand ticked past one o'clock. We still hadn't seen Mom.

"Maybe she already left and we missed her," suggested Mal.

"Even if she didn't, we could just sneak back in," offered Tamika.

"We can't risk it," I said. "If she spots us, we won't get away again."

Each minute seemed like an eternity as the clock passed 1:05, then 1:10.

"We're not going to have enough time!" said Mal.

Finally, at 1:12, Mom came out of the building. She was struggling to balance the picnic basket, beach umbrella, and lawn chairs in her arms. Something in my heart went twang, like a broken guitar string, as I watched her make her way down the sidewalk toward the intersection of Marine and Montrose.

I thought a lot about how much I missed Dad. And I'd even thought about how much she would miss Mal and me if we were gone. But suddenly I had an achy feeling as I thought about how much I'd miss her if *she* was gone.

"Can we go now?" asked Tamika, staring at my watch.

"Wait until she's out of sight," I said.

It took two more agonizing minutes before Mom was across Montrose, and then across Marine, and had disappeared under the Lake Shore Drive viaduct on her way to the beach.

We were already running by the time I said, "Now!"

◆ ◆ ◆

The moment the elevator doors slid open, I knew we were in trouble: The Phantom Tower was getting worse again. We stepped inside on a count of three so no one would chicken out, and as soon as we did, my skull was filled with the buzz of a radio stuck between stations. It was hard to think, but at least my insides weren't being whipped up for an omelet.

We searched apartment 1304 for Teddy, but it was empty and eerily silent. The endless dance party upstairs seemed to have finally ended.

Without saying a word, we headed down to the lobby.

It was total chaos. The residents of the Phantom Tower had gathered in the lobby like passengers on a sinking ship—some shouting, some crying, others praying quietly to themselves. Unlike a sinking ship, however, the Phantom Tower didn't have any lifeboats.

"We need to find Teddy!" I shouted above the racket, leading Mal and Tamika to the basement. We ran for the boiler room and didn't stop until we were in Teddy's clubhouse. If we didn't find him there, I didn't know where to look next.

At first, the room seemed empty. But as my lungs heaved—and I wondered why I couldn't feel the floor under my feet—I saw movement on the bed.

"Look!" said Tamika.

Teddy *was* there, lying on his back with his hands behind his head and flickering like a candle in a drafty room.

We moved closer, and he sat up, fading in so slowly that it took me a minute to see how sad he looked.

"I thought you were never coming back," he said. Then he saw our swimsuits and added: "Are you planning to go swimming?"

I shook my head. "Sorry it took so long. Things have been getting a little bit crazy on the outside."

As I quickly explained what we'd learned about the Professor, the Princess, and their parents, Teddy didn't look as interested as I thought he would. Then again, when he faded out he practically disappeared, so it was hard to tell what he was thinking.

When I finished, he stood up, walked over to the doorway, and looked out.

"So when the curse is lifted," he said, "you'll be free to live wherever you want, and you won't have to come here when you die."

"We think so," said Tamika.

"And what will happen to me?" he asked without turning around.

"We think you'll probably just go *poof*," said Mal.

Sometimes Mal makes me so mad that even punching him in the face wouldn't make me feel better. He had a lot to learn about how to talk to people—and ghosts, too.

"Unfortunately," I added, glaring at Mal, "if we *don't* lift the curse, and the Professor dies, we *all* go *poof*. And if the Professor recovers, he's going to try to make the curse last forever. If he can't do it with us, he's going to find another pair of twins, I just know it."

Teddy didn't move or say anything for a minute. Tamika and I just looked at each other. If we lifted the curse, he'd never see us again. If we didn't lift it and the Professor failed, he'd never see *anyone* again. He'd just disappear along with the rest of us. But if the Professor succeeded—well, I couldn't blame Teddy if he wanted the curse to go on forever.

Tamika crossed the room to Teddy. She tried to pat him on the back, but her hand went right through him, so instead she patted the place where it looked like his shoulder started.

Teddy noticed what she was doing and smiled. He turned around and gave her a hug, which made her shiver like someone had put snow down her neck.

"I guess I'd understand if you didn't want to help us," I told him.

"Well, I'd miss the three of you," said Teddy, "but to tell the truth, I am getting tired of living here. If you lift the curse, at least I get to look forward to something different, even if I don't know what it is."

"We don't know what's next, do we?" asked Tamika. "It might be nothing, or it might be something else. After all, we never knew this place existed."

Teddy smiled. "I'll find out, I guess."

"I hate to say this, but we need to keep moving," I said, glancing at Dad's watch.

"If Bricklayer John is the guy who built the Phantom Tower, that must be his apartment on the extra floor—the eighteenth," said Mal.

Teddy nodded.

"When he was alive, Vincent Krayfish lived on the top floor of Brunhild Tower," said Tamika. "So maybe he lives on the seventeenth floor here?"

"Apparently, he had jet-black hair with a white stripe," I added.

Teddy faded in, for a moment looking almost solid enough to touch. "Which one do you want to meet first?"

CHAPTER TWENTY-EIGHT

BRICKLAYER JOHN

TIME SEEMED TO ACCELERATE as we exited the flickering elevator on the seventeenth floor and climbed the shifting stairs to the eighteenth, where we hoped to find Bricklayer John. We had half an hour before the portal to Brunhild Tower closed for the day.

Teddy reached the door first, but instead of knocking, he stepped aside and looked at me. I was right behind him, and a glance at Mal and Tamika told me neither of them wanted to trade places with me.

I raised my hand, made a fist, and rapped on the door.

Heavy footfalls approached rapidly. Then the door opened, and a big man in overalls looked out at us with worry and surprise.

I recognized him right away from the newspaper photo. Up close, Bricklayer John looked so strong it was easy to imagine him swinging a load of bricks up onto a scaffold and mortaring them into place from dawn to dusk. His face looked rough and weathered from working outside during his short life, but his expression was gentle.

"I was expecting my son," he said, scanning our faces. "Who are you?"

None of us said anything as we pondered how to ask Bricklayer John for the thing that would keep him from seeing his son forever. We had a lot to tell him, not much time to say it, and no idea which words to use.

"We know John Junior, and we need to talk to you," I said finally.

Frowning, he stepped aside to let us in. As we passed through a long reception hall into an enormous living room with endless views of the twilit phantom world, I noticed that the apartment's decorations were very plain. Either Bricklayer John didn't have the imagination to fill his huge home with rich people's things or he was more comfortable with simple wood furniture, braided rugs, and plain white walls.

But just like the rest of the tower, the invisible glue that held it together was dissolving.

"John Junior comes at the same time every day, and we visit for an hour," said Bricklayer John, running his fingers through his dark, shaggy hair. "But he hasn't shown up for two days, and from the looks on your faces, he's not coming today, either."

Just then, the whole apartment seemed to blink slowly, and I had that nauseous feeling like my insides were in a blender. Mal and Tamika gasped—they felt it, too—as Bricklayer John calmly offered us chairs.

"I built this place as well as I could," he said, "but I'm starting to think it won't last forever."

I couldn't get over the fact that we were staring at Professor Parker's *dad*, who appeared to be a young man in his twenties, while the Professor himself was apparently dying of old age in a hospital bed.

"I don't know how to say this . . . ," began Tamika.

"We're really sorry," I added.

"But we're running out of time," blurted Mal, and before I could stop him he laid out the horrible facts in a sentence that felt like a hammer blow. "Your son is dying, and if he dies before lifting the curse, you and everyone here will disappear forever, and so will everyone living in Brunhild Tower, so we need your help lifting the curse—even though it means you'll never see your son again."

Bricklayer John took the hit without flinching, but he did finally sit down. Silhouetted against the soft violet light from the windows, only flickering once or twice, he looked like a statue.

"You do know about the curse, right?" asked Tamika softly.

"Yes, of course," said Bricklayer John, his voice getting husky as his shoulders slumped slightly. "My son has explained everything. My grandmother loved me, but love made her blind. By punishing Vincent Krayfish for taking my life, she also punished me and everyone who ever lived, or will live, in Brunhild Tower. John Junior spent his life trying to learn how to lift the curse, but he never learned the secret."

The Professor was a world-class liar—he was so good, I almost admired him.

"Oh, he learned how, all right," I told Bricklayer John. "But the real purpose of his research was exactly the opposite: to figure out how to make the curse go on even after he died. Then he planned to move into Brunhild Tower so he could be with you forever."

"He knows how to lift the curse?" asked Bricklayer John, clearly having a hard time taking this all in.

I nodded.

"But he loves you too much to let you go," said Tamika.

"If you ask me, that's just selfish," said Mal.

I poked him just under the ribs with two fingers. Maybe it was, but he was talking about the man's son. Mal pretended it didn't hurt.

Bricklayer John turned to Teddy. "You haven't said anything, young man."

Teddy looked glum. "I'm like you. I can't come and go like my friends. I'm just thinking how much I'll miss them."

"But you think we should help them?"

Flickering rapidly, Teddy blew a small bubble and chewed it with a series of pops. "Mal may be rude, but he's right: It's selfish not to. I would have lived my life outside the tower if I'd had the chance. And why should we hang on to the people we care about until we all disappear?"

Teddy's words made me realize the dead and the living both had a hard time letting go. If it was my dad in the Phantom Tower, I might have been as bad as the Professor.

Bricklayer John stood up, walked to a window, and looked out.

"I have been fortunate to be so loved, though that love for me has hurt many others," he said. "I only wish I had a chance to tell my son goodbye."

"We can tell him for you," said Tamika, her voice barely more than a whisper.

Bricklayer John gave a small nod and turned around to face us.

"You must lift the curse," he said. "If I die a second time, we will at least restore the natural order, for a son should never die before his father. Tell John Junior I love him and I want him to enjoy the rest of his life without me."

Relief swelled in my chest.

"Now, what do you need from me?" asked Bricklayer John.

"A piece of clothing, and fast," said Mal.

He sat down again and unlaced one of his tall work boots. Tugging the boot by the heel until it came off, he rolled down a red wool sock, slipped it off, and handed it to Mal.

From the look on his face and the way he tried to hold it without really touching it, I could tell exactly what Mal was thinking: *Great, a hundred-year-old sock.*

Tamika and I thanked Bricklayer John and got up, hoping we didn't look rude. Outside the windows, the Phantom Tower's aurora rippled and bent like the Northern Lights, one time flashing brightly enough to make us wince.

I spotted an old clock on the mantel, its hands at 1:47.

"Is that time correct?" I asked.

"It should be," said Bricklayer John. "My son winds and sets it regularly to be sure he won't stay too long."

"Thirteen minutes, guys," I told Mal, Tamika, and Teddy. "And we still need to see Vincent Krayfish."

"Where does he live?" asked Tamika.

Bricklayer John gave a small smile. "Why, the Krayfishes live just downstairs."

CHAPTER TWENTY-NINE

PRINCESS VIVIAN AND VINCENT KRAYFISH

BRICKLAYER JOHN WATCHED from the doorway with his hand raised in silent farewell as we hurried downstairs.

"That went pretty well, all things considered," said Tamika.

"But why did he have to give us a *sock?*" moaned Mal, who'd gotten stuck carrying it. "It could have been his belt, or his jacket, or even his shirt."

"Look on the bright side," I told him. "He could have given us an old pair of underwear."

Mal shuddered and stopped complaining.

"I don't think we're going to be so lucky with Mr. Krayfish," said Teddy as we arrived at the door to 1704. "He rarely leaves his apartment, and when he does, he's mean as a polecat. Nobody likes him—not even his wife."

"I'm sure he can't be that bad," said Tamika hopefully.

Once again, nobody wanted to knock, so I did it.

"*What?*" snarled Vincent Krayfish as he yanked his door open.

"That bad," whispered Mal behind me.

Krayfish was wearing a silk bathrobe over a shirt and tie, and his glossy, ink-black hair had a white stripe, just like in the photo. His mustache was so thin it looked like it had been drawn on with a pencil.

Seeing Teddy, he said in a voice dripping with sarcasm, "Oh look, it's the boy who couldn't swim." Then when he noticed Mal and I were wearing swimsuits, he added, "I guess the lifeguards were off duty for you, too?"

"I can see why nobody likes you," Tamika observed.

"Is that supposed to make me feel bad?" snapped Krayfish. "Well, boo-hoo-hoo. I guess I'll go spend eternity in a cell made for two—oh wait! Too late!"

"Who ees eet?" called a voice that sounded almost exactly like the Princess in full princess mode.

"Nobody, *darling*," said Krayfish over his shoulder. "Just some solicitors—and they're already on their way."

He tried to slam the door, but I stuck out my foot and stopped it from closing.

Krayfish gaped. "You insolent brat!"

"Help me," I said, and Teddy, Tamika, and Mal pushed forward, putting their shoulders against the door until we were able to barge past Vincent Krayfish.

A woman who was the spitting image of the Princess, only a couple of decades younger, came around the corner as we crowded into the reception hall: Princess Vivian. Apparently, she remembered herself as a middle-aged woman, while her husband was a mirror image of himself just days before he died.

"I knew you ver lyink," she said in disgust. "There never has been a solicitor een thees godforsaken place. But I vud velcome the Fuller Brush salesman vith open arms: He vud be more interestink to talk to than you!"

"You're no picnic yourself, Princess," said Krayfish. "At least you could have come back from the dead looking like you did when we first met, not some haggard hausfrau!"

"Alas. Eef I had only looked thees way then, you never vud have vooed me," moaned the Princess.

These two should welcome an end to the curse, I thought. The past decades had clearly been torture for them both.

"We don't have time for this," said Tamika.

I decided they probably didn't need to hear the whole story—and we were going to do them both a huge favor, anyway.

"If you don't want to be trapped here forever, you have to help us," I said. "All we need is a piece of your clothing."

Krayfish looked at us coldly, then spoke over his shoulder as he turned and walked out. "My wardrobe is off-limits. Now beat it! I'm going to work on my stamp collection."

We chased after him with the Princess following behind.

"Look around you," I told him. "You can see for yourself the tower is coming apart."

"No, it isn't," said Krayfish, ignoring the fact that the hallway was expanding and contracting like an accordion.

I staggered as an energy wave surged through me, and I could tell Mal and Tamika were feeling it, too. The clock was ticking, and Vincent Krayfish obviously wasn't going to change his mind anytime soon.

Still, we followed him down the hall into what would have been, in our apartment, Mal's and my bedroom, only here it was a study with a large desk and books lining the walls.

"How did you get all these books in here?" asked Tamika, book-crazy under any circumstances.

"How should I know?" snapped Krayfish as he sat down behind the desk and opened a large stamp album. "Bricklayer John handled everything. He's not the sharpest tool in the shed, but he gets things done."

"You're lucky he lets you live here at all, after what you did," I said.

"Bricklayer John has made the best of thinks," said the Princess, coming into the room behind us. "Thanks to his grandmother's curse, neither he nor I can evict the unpleasant Mr. Krayfish."

Krayfish smoothed his tie and grinned. "And you'd like to do that, wouldn't you, doll? Sorry, but you're going to be putting up with me for millennia. Now scram, kids."

Ignoring us, he picked up a pair of tweezers in one hand and a magnifying glass in the other and began examining a small triangular stamp.

I looked at Mal and Tamika to see if they had any ideas, but the expressions on their faces didn't give me any hope. Teddy was barely there, and the Princess looked sadder than any of us. She clearly regretted marrying Vincent Krayfish—and now a curse kept her from ever leaving him.

"I'm sorry your daughter got caught up in all of this," Tamika said to Princess Vivian. "She's been really nice to us."

The Princess looked at her husband cautiously. Opening a drawer and using her body to shield it from Krayfish's view, she took out a long pair of scissors and offered them to us.

"My daughter vill not end up trapped here vith *him* as I haff been," she whispered. "Take these."

Teddy was the first to understand. Grabbing the scissors, he said, "Wow, look at all these books!" and wandered behind the desk. Then, standing behind Krayfish, he lifted the stamp collector's tie with one hand and snipped it off with the other.

"Why, you little—"

But Teddy was on the other side of the room before the red-faced Krayfish was out of his chair.

"Run!" he yelled, and he didn't have to say it twice. We barreled down the hallway and out the front door while the Princess yelled, "Good luck!" behind us and Krayfish howled and raged.

The stairs were turning in a slow spiral, forcing me to hold on to the handrail and bend my knees for balance as we made our way down. Mal yelped, and I turned around just in time to see him falling toward me. Bracing myself for impact, I held on for dear life as we collided and then teetered toward the stairwell. If we fell, we were going over the edge and all the way to the bottom. Teddy could only look on helplessly.

Then I heard Tamika grunt like a professional tennis player serving a ball. Wrapping her arms around Mal's chest, she pulled him off me, and we all fell back onto the stairs.

"Lost my footing," said Mal shakily. "Thanks, guys."

"No problem, brother," I said.

"I've got your backs," said Tamika. "Now let's keep moving."

When we reached the fourteenth floor, we barged into the elevator lobby.

"I hope the elevator still works," said Mal as he pressed the button.

Teddy put the piece of Krayfish's tie in my hand, and I closed my fingers around it.

"Good luck, and hurry," he said.

Above the elevator, the floor indicators moved with painful slowness as the elevator climbed up from below.

"This *elevator* needs to hurry," grumbled Mal.

"Thank you for everything, Teddy," said Tamika. "We'll never, ever forget you. You will live on in our memories for as long as we're alive."

I could tell she wanted to hug him, and he would have liked to be hugged, but they both knew her arms would go right through him. Teddy shrugged and smiled. Then he took out his bubble gum and stuck it behind his ear.

"I've been saving my second stick of gum for eighty-four

years," he said, reaching in his pocket. "I might as well have it now!"

As he unwrapped the fresh piece and popped it in his mouth, two things happened at once: The elevator door opened with a *DING*, and the stairwell door flew open with a *BANG*. Vincent Krayfish, his robe flapping and his sawed-off tie dangling, lunged at me.

"GIVE ME THAT!" he shouted.

I jumped back, but I wasn't fast enough. Krayfish grabbed the tie and yanked it out of my fingers.

Mal made a fist and swung, trying to give him the mother of all dead arms, but his punch whistled straight through the ghostly real-estate developer, unfortunately hitting Tamika on the other side.

"OW!" she yelled.

Teddy pulled back his leg and kicked Krayfish in the shin so hard he howled in pain. *We* may not have been able to touch the spirits in the Phantom Tower, but clearly they were real to each other.

Krayfish stayed on his feet and made a fist, preparing to swing at Teddy. I darted in, grabbed the tie with both hands, and pulled with all my strength.

"Help me!" I said.

Tamika put her hands over mine on the tie, and Mal wrapped his arms around my waist, trying to help me win the tug-of-war.

We should have won. But Krayfish's strength was superhuman—and so was the foot-long piece of silk tie.

"You lousy kids have no idea what you're meddling with," spat Krayfish.

"Actually, we do," said Tamika through gritted teeth.

As Teddy hauled back his leg to kick again, Krayfish smiled a slow, superior smile and, with a mighty yank, pulled the tie out of our hands.

Tamika, Mal, and I tumbled backward into the elevator just as the doors slid shut, leaving Teddy outside in the elevator lobby.

"Do we have the tie?" asked Mal, who had pressed the button for our floor while we were fighting with Krayfish.

"Not even a thread of it," I groaned as the elevator started moving downward.

"At least I still have Bricklayer John's sock," said Mal, taking it out of his pocket.

But when the doors opened, we didn't see the familiar pictures of old Chicago—instead we saw framed pictures of birds and blue-and-silver wallpaper.

I looked at the watch on my wrist: 2:01.

The portal to Brunhild Tower had closed.

We were trapped in the Phantom Tower.

CHAPTER THIRTY

THE STUFF THE UNIVERSE IS MADE OF

WE FOUND TEDDY on the seventeenth floor, banging on Vincent Krayfish's door with both hands.

"Open up!" he yelled. "Give my friends that tie or I'll . . . I'll—"

"Or you'll what?" came Krayfish's muffled voice.

"Or I'll knock this door down, and you won't like what happens next!" said Teddy, his voice losing confidence with each word.

His shoulders slumped as he turned around, leaned against the door, and slid down to the floor. Then he saw us.

"Oh no," said Teddy.

"We're stuck here until tomorrow," Tamika told him, confirming what he must have already known.

Teddy pointed back at the door with his thumb. "I chased him up here, but he locked the door before I could catch him. And now there's no way in."

"That's what I've been telling you!" cackled Krayfish behind the door.

"I told you all this was hopeless," said Mal, "but nobody listened."

As the Phantom Tower continued to ripple and shimmy, the door somehow stayed tight in its frame. I turned the handle and yanked on it, but Teddy was right: It was locked.

He was wrong about something else, though.

There was definitely a way in.

• • •

Bricklayer John didn't say a word as he opened his door, but he didn't have to: The expression on his face did it for him.

"You didn't expect us back so soon, did you?" I asked as the four of us filed past him into his apartment.

He shook his head. "What happened?"

Bricklayer John's face darkened as we told him what happened with Vincent Krayfish and his tie. It was like a fast-moving cloud covering a bright full moon. "I see now I expected too much of him," he said. "I assumed he would see the sense of what you're saying and that he would help you of his own free will."

"And how long have you known him?" asked Mal sarcastically.

Just as quickly, the cloud passed and Bricklayer John laughed. "It has always been a failing of mine to expect the best of others."

"I don't think that's a failing," said Tamika.

"Well, it's a little unrealistic," I said, and Tamika elbowed me in the ribs.

"Wait here," Bricklayer John told us.

He was only gone a moment, and when he came back, he was carrying a small wooden toolbox and wearing a look of grim determination. We followed him downstairs to Krayfish's door and stood back while he smacked it three times with an open hand.

"KRAYFISH!" he roared. "OPEN UP!"

There was no sneering answer this time. In fact, there was no answer at all.

Bricklayer John set down his toolbox and took out a short, wood-handled hammer with a broad, flat head. He squared his feet and sized up the wall.

"I prefer to work with a trowel," he said. "To build things, not break them. But every tool has its time and purpose."

What happened next is the kind of thing that's hard to describe because we don't have words for it, maybe because nobody ever sees it.

When you place or mine bricks in *Minecraft*, they just appear or disappear, and it's no big deal: They're either there or they're not. But when Bricklayer John hit the wall with his hammer, it was the total opposite of no big deal. It didn't disappear, and it didn't crumble like it would in the real world, either.

Instead there was this flowing, wavy light as the wall bent and shifted. Bricklayer John kept swinging the hammer, and every time it hit, the wall opened a little more. Inside the wall, there wasn't plaster and lathe or bricks and mortar: There were swirly, rainbow-colored particles that seemed less like building materials than the stuff the universe was made of.

He kept working until there was a hole big enough to climb through. We could see down the front hall of the apartment, all the way to a wide-eyed Vincent Krayfish peeping around the corner of the living room.

Bricklayer John lowered his hammer. "I could make the work neater, but if you are right, we won't be around long enough to require any finishing touches."

He looked tired, and I realized even that short burst of work had required a lot of energy. How much must it have taken to build the entire Phantom Tower over all those years?

We followed him through the hole, into the reception hall, and around the corner to the living room, where Krayfish was cowering in the farthest corner as light pulsed outside the windows behind him.

"You really know how to hold on to a grudge," said Krayfish nervously as the usually peaceful Bricklayer John stalked toward him. "Look, I apologize: I'm sorry I killed you. Does that make you feel better?"

Bricklayer John kept coming.

"I know my dear wife was right and I should have said something sooner, but somehow I just never got around to it," babbled Krayfish.

Bricklayer John opened his left hand and reached out to accept the tie.

Vincent Krayfish looked over his right shoulder, but there was nowhere for him to go—except, I suddenly realized, out.

"The window!" I shouted at the exact same moment that Krayfish turned, raised the sash, and leaned out.

In life, he had jumped off the top of a building to escape his responsibilities—in death, he was trying to do the same thing. And here it probably wouldn't even hurt.

Bricklayer John dropped his hammer and took three quick steps. Grabbing Krayfish securely by the back of his robe and the seat of his pants, he hauled him inside and stood him on his feet, blocking the window with his own body.

"Give it to them," he commanded.

I walked up and held out my hand. Sulking, Krayfish gave me the piece of his tie.

"You really need to learn to let things go," he said.

"But that's exactly the point," answered Bricklayer John. "I have."

◆ ◆ ◆

I had barely closed my fingers around the tie when the whole room contracted three times in a row, leaving me feeling like someone had stuffed me in a garbage can and rolled me down a hill. Mal and Tamika looked like they felt the same way. I could tell the ghosts felt something, too, but they looked more confused than hurt.

I rolled the tie and jammed it in my pocket, just in case Krayfish suddenly decided to take it back.

"I think John Junior isn't doing well," groaned Tamika after the energy wave subsided.

"He must hold on one more day if you are to see your parents again," said Bricklayer John. "Now, come with me."

We followed. After seeing him bust through that wall, we would have followed him anywhere in the Phantom Tower.

Back upstairs in his apartment, we sat down again while Bricklayer John paced restlessly, his eyes on the shifting, warping, disintegrating features of his building.

"It must be difficult to see your hard work falling apart," Mal surprised me by saying. "It took you so many years to build. I've only made things in *Minecraft*, but I know how mad it makes me when Colm ruins my work."

Filling some rooms with cats or chickens wasn't the same thing as ruining someone's life's work, but I didn't bother defending myself. Mal was right.

Bricklayer John stopped, ran his fingers through his hair, and laughed. "Look at me, worrying like a landlord. I suppose I should just enjoy myself. It is hard to see the building go, but nothing lasts forever, whether it's us or the things we build."

Tamika leaned forward. "Why don't you know how everything works, when you built this all from nothing?"

"When I woke up in this place, I didn't know why I was here or what had happened. I didn't even know I was dead until Krayfish showed up and explained it all to me. We kept our distance. But I was a builder in life and found I could make things here, too. I felt like I still had work to do. As others started to join us, they needed a place to stay, so I began to build the north tower as well as I could remember it."

"You remembered really well," said Mal. "I hope I can be half as good a builder as you are."

Bricklayer John smiled. "It's going to be a long night, I'm afraid. Since you're all stuck here anyway, would you like to see something truly unusual?"

"It's hard to imagine anything more unusual than this," I told him.

He smiled. "You might be surprised."

◆ ◆ ◆

Everyone in the lobby was really freaking out now, but Bricklayer John led us calmly through the crowd and through the front doors, where right away my head stopped feeling like it was going to explode.

"It's nicer out here," marveled Tamika at the calm, quiet twilight. "Why doesn't everyone just come outside?"

Bricklayer John strode ahead, leaving the grounds of the building and heading toward the lake. "When a ship is sinking, the passengers don't immediately throw themselves into the water. They stay on until the last minute, hoping for rescue, which is actually a very reasonable thing to do."

In the real world, the lake was about a half mile away, but here, it was only a few hundred yards.

"Why is the lake so close?" I asked.

"It used to be like this a long time ago," said Tamika. "But the city has gradually been filling in the lake to make more land."

"Is that so?" asked Bricklayer John curiously. "I do wish I could see that."

The shoreline looked marshy from a distance, but up close it seemed unfinished. The ground under our feet wasn't wet or muddy or sandy—it felt like walking on a deep shag carpet.

"What did you want to show us?" asked Mal.

"Turn around," said Bricklayer John.

We gasped. To the south, west, and north, there were towers, spires, and steeples of an entire phantom city. There were old buildings, and new buildings, and buildings that had been built in between. Some of them stood side by side, but many of them overlapped like they had been built on the exact same lot.

And not all the buildings looked like the kind you'd see in the real world, either. Some were strangely shaped, curved like horns or wings, or designed like plants so they seemed like growing things. Many were so delicate I didn't know how they could keep from falling down. With lanterns, and gaslights, and electric lights, and light sources that couldn't possibly have been invented yet, the skyline was intricate and dizzying, like a whole galaxy set down gently on earth.

In front of the phantom skyline, the Phantom Tower stood tall with lights burning in every window and a multicolored energy storm swirling around it like a soft-hued rainbow tornado.

"I believe this is all the Chicagos that have ever been or will be," said Bricklayer John. "It's never been this bright before."

Tamika sighed, the way you sigh when you see something so wonderful that words will only ruin it.

"It's beautiful," said Mal.

But his words didn't ruin it. It still was.

• • •

We spent the night on the beach of Phantom Lake Michigan, watching the light show against the glittering, filigree skyline of Phantom Chicago, wondering if at any moment the tower would wink out of existence and we would, too.

But it didn't, and we didn't, so we murmured and dozed and thought and worried. I had a hard time sleeping because I was so hungry, but there was no food anywhere. Thinking of food reminded me of Mom: I kept picturing her walking up and down the beach with her picnic basket, calling our names and not finding us anywhere. And there was no way to tell her where we were—next door and a million miles away. Tamika's parents would be worried sick, too, knowing even less about where their daughter had gone.

And how was the Professor? Was he sleeping peacefully, or getting ready to draw his final breath?

We all wished we could make time go faster, but none of us wanted to say it—we didn't really know what came next for Bricklayer John, Teddy, and all the souls of the Phantom Tower, but these moments were probably their last.

I just hoped they weren't our last, too.

CHAPTER THIRTY-ONE

A WIND FROM NOWHERE

THE NEXT DAY, the waves of energy swirling around the Phantom Tower had subsided slightly, although Phantom Chicago was just as bright as before. We made our way back inside, ready to leave the moment the portal opened. Bricklayer John and Teddy came along to see us off.

"Tell my son I love him, and we will never truly be parted," said Bricklayer John. "Even if the memories fade, our souls will always remain connected."

"You could have been the best friends I ever had—I wish I'd had time to find out," said Teddy.

"We'll never forget either one of you," I told them. "Someday we'll tell the world your story."

"The world would never believe it," said Mal.

"Maybe they would if we pretended it was fiction," said Tamika. "I just might write it myself."

We stepped into the elevator. Looking at the piece of Krayfish's tie in my hand and Bricklayer John's sock in

Mal's, I hoped the phantom clothes wouldn't disappear the second we left the Phantom Tower.

Mal pushed the button, and we all waved goodbye as the doors closed. We didn't speak while the elevator made its short drop.

As soon as the doors opened and we saw the pictures of old Chicago, I felt a huge sense of relief, knowing we were back in Brunhild Tower. The tie and sock were still in our hands, although the tie felt weird, like it had millipede legs all wiggling in different directions.

But when I saw Mom—frozen with her key in the lock of our door, her face pale with shock at the sight of us—that relief turned to cold fear.

She wasn't mad at first. Leaving her key ring hanging, she wrapped all three of us in a fierce hug that practically made us fall back into the elevator. Tears poured down her face as she kissed us, including Tamika, and said, "You're back," over and over again.

Then, finally, when she got control of herself, she wiped her cheeks and asked, "Are you okay? Where have you *been*?"

"We're fine, Mrs. McShane," said Tamika while I tried to decide how to handle it.

"I've been so worried! At first I thought you drowned," said Mom. "But after I interrogated every lifeguard on the beach, and none of them had seen twin boys, I started to think you were *kidnapped*. I called the police, Malcolm. Tamika's parents and I have been up *all night*."

As she talked, I could hear anger wrestling with her sense of relief, and I knew I was one wrong word away from a full-scale eruption of Mount Furious.

"We're sor—" Mal tried to say, but Mom cut him off.

Sorry was the wrong word. Because *sorry* meant we'd done something wrong.

"Sorry? SORRY?!? You may THINK you're sorry, but you WILL be sorry if you don't have an EXPLANATION for WHAT you were DOING. Though I can't think of a single reason you could have for disappearing for the last twenty-four hours and scaring me and Mr. and Mrs. Jackson to death!"

I didn't say anything as she opened the door to our apartment.

"Inside, all of you," Mom told us. "After I call Tamika's parents, I'm going to call the police and tell them you're safe. Then you can explain yourselves to all of us."

Tamika followed us inside. While Mom closed the door, she turned, cleared her throat, and said, "You should definitely call the police, Mrs. McShane. We didn't run away, but that's what you should tell them. We'll tell *you* the truth."

Mom looked confused. "If you didn't run away, then why should I say you did? What's going on here?"

That's when I realized Tamika was right. It was time to stop lying.

"This is going to sound made-up," I began, "but it's not. Mom, please try to keep an open mind."

• • •

Mr. and Mrs. Jackson made it to our apartment in about two minutes flat. And, after they went through the same stages of relief, suspicion, and anger as Mom, they finally agreed to hear us out. Naturally, the telling-the-truth part didn't go well—I should have known they wouldn't believe us.

Mal and Tamika had both agreed that I should do the talking because I was the best storyteller. It was either a super nice thing to say or a brilliant way of avoiding responsibility, but I decided to take it as a compliment. Our parents sat down in the living room and listened openmouthed as I told them everything, starting at the beginning: from meeting the Princess to discovering the thirteenth floor, from hanging out with Teddy and hiding from the Professor to what happened at the University of Chicago.

That's when Mom clapped a hand to her mouth. "That was *you*?" she whispered. "But the witnesses said there were only two kids."

"I was already downstairs," said Mal sheepishly.

"We did not raise you to behave like this, young lady," Mr. Jackson told Tamika sternly.

"We didn't mean to hurt anyone," Tamika said. "Please just wait for the rest of the story."

I took a deep breath and kept going. The grown-ups all frowned at the part where we went to visit the Professor with the Princess, and shook their heads at the part where Mal took a blood sample from the Princess, but at least they didn't interrupt.

By the time I got to Vincent Krayfish and Bricklayer John, though, I could tell I was losing them. Earlier, Mom had been looking at Mal and Tamika like she was trying to see if they believed my crazy story, too. But while I told everybody about Bricklayer John breaking into Krayfish's apartment, and the glittering skyline of Chicagos past, present, and future, the look on her face hurt worse than anything: She was embarrassed of me.

Even when I was making stuff up after Dad died, I had never made up anything as crazy as this. As the story went on, she just started looking depressed, like my mind had snapped and she didn't know what to do about it.

When I was finally done, Mom turned to Mr. and Mrs. Jackson and said, "I am so, so sorry."

"We're sorry, too," said Mrs. Jackson. "Tamika clearly bears just as much responsibility as your boys."

"You're acting like this is all our fault!" I said, my head getting hot. "You should be thanking us for trying to save you!"

Mom stood up and put her hand on my arm. "Colm, honey, I know this move has been hard for you. And we're all still hurting after what happened to your dad. But you can't cover up what really happened by distracting us with even wilder stories."

"I'm not making anything—"

"Mom," said Mal, interrupting and putting *his* hand on *her* arm. "I know this is hard to believe."

"That's putting it mildly," muttered Mr. Jackson.

"You're right, Mal," said Mom. "And in fact, I *don't* believe it."

"I don't blame you," said Mal. "Colm, Tamika, and I have had time to let it sink in and you're hearing it for the first time."

"And I hope this is the last time we hear it," added Mrs. Jackson.

"Mom, Dad, Mrs. McShane," said Tamika, "this isn't just Colm's story. All three of us have seen the same things, and we even have an adult who can vouch for us: the Princess."

"We will not involve some nice old lady in this . . . fantasy," said Mom, a little less sure of herself.

Eric jumped up onto the arm of the couch and nuzzled me. I scratched his head and could feel the vibrations of his purring in his neck.

"You don't have to take our word for it, or even the Princess's," I said. "Because we can prove it."

"If we're wrong, you can punish us however you want," added Mal. "But you're going to be glad when you find out we're right."

I was grateful to have Mal on my side, but it was such a new experience I didn't know how to show my gratitude. So, I hit him.

"Ow!" he said, rubbing his arm. "What was that for?"

"Just my way of saying thanks, brother," I told him sincerely.

"Well, you're welcome. Don't thank me again."

◆ ◆ ◆

It took another hour to convince the grown-ups, but finally we were riding south on Lake Shore Drive in the minivan, with Mom at the wheel and the Princess riding shotgun while Mal and I sat in the back. When I turned around and looked out the back window, I could see Mr. and Mrs. Jackson in the car behind us. We asked them to let Tamika ride with us, but they said they needed some family time.

I was glad Dante wasn't driving our car because, even with Mom's nerves stretched tight as ukulele strings, she was at least hitting the speed limit.

Mom kept glancing over at the Princess and asking if she was comfortable. I think she was embarrassed by our van: It needed washing and vacuuming and still smelled like stale cheeseburgers.

"Eet ees quite comfortable, thank you," said the Princess in her princess voice.

◆ ◆ ◆

As soon as our cars were parked in the hospital garage, Mal, Tamika, and I jumped out and headed for the hospital door, leaving our parents to follow along with the Princess. We waited for them outside the Professor's room: They arrived looking like they couldn't believe we'd talked them into coming this far, but now it was too late to turn back. We went in before they could change their minds.

"Oh great, you brought your parents," sneered the Professor as we entered.

"How are you feeling, Professor Parker?" asked Mom meekly.

His bed was raised so he was almost sitting up, but he put his hand on his heart, made a pitiful face, and groaned.

"We're very sorry to disturb you," said Mom. "In fact, I can't even believe we're here—but the children insisted. They've told us the most . . . *remarkable* . . . story."

When the Professor realized Mom didn't believe us, his eyes lit up.

"And what story is this?" he asked. "Did they tell you how they broke into my office and took something very important to me?"

Mom glared at us. "Whatever they really did, I assure you they will face appropriate consequences."

The Professor leaned back. "That is the only story that matters here. Take them away and punish them—spare not the rod!—and I'll be happy to say no more about it."

Mr. and Mrs. Jackson looked at each other like, *Did he just suggest we beat the children?* I knew Mom would never do that, but she might lock up every electronic device in the house.

"Maybe we should go," said Mrs. Jackson softly.

The Princess cleared her throat. "Ve are not goink anyvair!"

"At least not until you hear what your father had to say," added Tamika.

That caught the Professor by surprise. "You . . . saw my father?"

"He said he loves you and he wants you to enjoy the rest of your life without him, but you're supposed to help us lift the curse," I told him.

"You're lying," muttered the Professor. "My father loves me too much to just . . . let me go."

"Maybe he said that *because* he loves you," said Mal, which surprised me because he's usually clueless about emotional stuff.

"He also said a son should never die before his father," I added.

Out of the corner of my eye, I saw Mom put her hand on her heart. She blinked like she was holding back tears.

The Professor thought about what we'd said and then shook his head. "Even if my father did say that, he wasn't thinking clearly. I will not help you break my great-grandmother's spell."

Mom and Tamika's parents all looked at him like they'd just heard Neil deGrasse Tyson say magic is real. The Professor had just confirmed the existence of the curse.

I stepped forward. "Actually, we don't need your help," I informed him. "We figured out how to do it—with a little help from your notebook."

"*Give my notebook back,*" growled the Professor.

Mom's eyebrows furrowed. "Did you take that from his office? Malcolm, that's stealing!"

"Just wait, Mom," said Mal.

While our parents shook their heads and murmured, we showed the Professor the things we'd collected: the drops of the Princess's blood, the lock of Vincent Krayfish's hair, Bricklayer John's sock, and the piece of Krayfish's tie.

"And my father's hair? How do you plan to get that?" asked the Professor.

"He was a hairy man," said Mal, plucking some curly hairs from the antique sock and looking at them like he'd found them in a sandwich. "Your curse-breaking instructions didn't say the hairs had to be from his head."

"You still don't have the last thing you need—that is, unless you intend to stab me!" insisted the Professor with a meaningful look at Mom.

He was right. We couldn't exactly hold him down and take a blood sample with our parents in the room.

But Tamika was ahead of all of us. "That won't be necessary," she said, taking a vial of blood from a nearby nurse's cart and reading the label. "I see you recently had your blood drawn."

The Professor turned white and then red, his eyes bulging and his veins popping out as he lunged at us from his hospital bed.

Mr. Jackson stepped into the center of the room. "I don't pretend to know what is going on here—you almost had me believing this—but you kids need to stop torturing this delirious old man right now." He turned to his wife. "Janelle, call a nurse."

"YOU VILL NOT CALL A NURSE," commanded the Princess. "Eet ees the arrogance of adults to believe only those thinks they haff experienced themselves, as eef young people haff not seen thinks beyond our imagininks. Do you not trust your own children? Vell, eef you cannot believe your ears, then perhaps your eyes vill see clearly."

Mr. Jackson hesitated. The Princess was hard to resist.

"Proceed, children," intoned the Princess.

Mr. Jackson stepped back, and our shocked parents watched quietly while we assembled all the items listed in the Professor's notebook. Then, following Tamika's instructions, we wrapped them in a piece of paper and put them in a metal bowl on the floor. They finally may have been as curious to see where things were going as the rest of us.

"You stole that! *Give it back!*" shouted the Professor as Tamika took out his field notes to the afterlife and turned to a page she'd marked with the ribbon.

Ignoring him, she started to read. The words were harsh and strange, written in a language I didn't recognize. But Tamika sounded them out carefully, speaking a clear voice that filled the room.

"Ve al la vivo!
Ĉar la vivo estas ve!
La malĝusta literumado!
Puni la malĝustan animon!"

The air suddenly chilled, like we'd stepped into a walk-in cooler, and Mom gasped and reached out to the Princess for support. The two of them put their arms around each other, and Mr. and Mrs. Jackson did the same, as the room fell silent. Except for Tamika's voice, we may as well have been floating in outer space. I couldn't hear the beeping of the bedside machines, the voices in the hallway outside, or the Professor's continued angry ranting. It was like my ears were plugged and I was hearing Tamika's voice directly in my brain.

"Prenu ĉi tiujn oferojn, diinon.
La sango de la vivantoj.
La haroj de la mortintoj.
Tio, kion ili portis.
De ĉi tiu mondo al la sekva."

I saw but couldn't hear Mom gasp when a thin blue light began swirling over the metal bowl. As if we were in the Phantom Tower again, the air felt charged with electricity and possibility. The sterile hospital room was a strange place to see magic—I wondered what the doctors in the halls would think if they happened to look in.

Then the spell of silence broke. It felt like my ears were popping as a wind rose from nowhere and flapped the curtains and the blankets of the Professor's bed.

"Stop, stop—please!" begged the Professor. "I need more time with my father!"

I felt sorry for him, and I knew how hard this had to be. I almost wanted to stop. But Bricklayer John was right: If the Professor really loved his dad, his dad would always be with him.

"Keep going, Tamika," I said.

Tamika nodded at me and didn't miss a beat, sounding out the strange-sounding words in a voice that was louder than before.

"*Mi donas al vi ĉi tion.*
Mi parolas ĉi tiujn vortojn.
Reversa la malbeno.
Vi antaŭe aŭdis.
Reversa la malbeno!
Reversa la malbeno!"

The wind grew stronger until it felt like a gale—we all held on to the Princess to keep her from being blown over—and then the room itself started to spin. Tamika shouted the words over the howling wind, and then the book was literally blown out of her hands and lost amid the other flying debris.

The floor and walls started quaking as the medical equipment swayed and clattered. Then there was a blinding flash of light, and somebody screamed—I think it was Mal.

While we blinked and waited for the spots in front of our eyes to go away, the wind stopped blowing, the floor stopped shaking, and everything returned to normal.

The Princess broke the silence first. "Vell, eef the old buzzard vasn't dead already, that should haff done the trick," she declared.

"Are you all right, Professor Parker?" asked Tamika, going to his side.

He actually did look a little bit better, as if a weight

had been lifted along with the curse. But he sure didn't want to admit it.

"I doubt I have long to live with this broken heart," muttered the Professor, turning away from her.

"So that's it? The curse is over?" Mal asked.

"I guess so," said Tamika, finding *Field Notes* in a corner and checking it for damage.

That's when I noticed our parents were frozen like figures in a wax museum. Their mouths were open, their eyes were wide, and their mind-melted expressions said, *That didn't just happen—did it?*

Finally, Mom moved. As she brushed her hair out of her face and tucked it behind her ear, I saw a strand of silver glint in the light. Had it just turned white, or had I only noticed it now?

"Do you believe me now, Mom?" I asked.

She looked me in the eye and nodded. I could tell she was about to go in for a hug.

"I believe you, Colm. And I'm sorry."

CHAPTER THIRTY-TWO

THE PARTING GLASS

MOM AND THE PRINCESS didn't talk much on the drive home, and I'm guessing it was a quiet ride in Tamika's car, too. When we left him, the Professor seemed more sad than angry. He told us he just wanted to be alone with his memories, and I understood him wanting to enjoy them while he could.

"I hope you're happy," he told us bitterly.

We weren't happy, and I still felt bad for him, but we were definitely relieved.

"I hope you get well soon," I said.

Before we left, our parents made us give his notebook back.

◆ ◆ ◆

It was evening when we finally pulled off Lake Shore Drive onto Montrose. Just as we were about to turn into Brunhild Tower, Mom hit the brakes in the middle of the road and screeched to a halt. Horns blared behind us, and one impatient driver revved his engine, squealed his tires, and zoomed into oncoming traffic to pass us.

"Look," she said, pointing ahead with a quivering arm.

We looked and stared in shock at what we saw.

The parking lot was in semidarkness, which at first glance seemed to be the shadow of our building. But it couldn't have been. For one, the sun was on the same side. And, as I looked up, I could see that the shadow was massive, tower-shaped, and two stories taller than Brunhild Tower.

"Oh no," I groaned.

Mom steered into the driveway and parked at the yellow gate to the parking lot, where the shade started as suddenly as a wall. The Jacksons pulled up behind us. We all jumped out of our cars.

The two buildings, mirror images of each other, would have formed a massive, soaring cliff. As it was, the outline of the Phantom Tower was just dark enough to dim the light from the dying sun. None of the people passing on the sidewalk seemed to notice—I guess in the evening light it was hard to see.

"What's going on?" Mal asked.

"Maybe we didn't lift the curse correctly," said Tamika.

Different possibilities crowded my skull. "What if it backfired and brought the Phantom Tower into the real world? Or . . . what if we're getting pulled into the phantom world?"

"Are we sure this isn't just a trick of the light?" asked Mrs. Jackson, shading her eyes against the sun.

Mr. Jackson put his hand on her shoulder. "I see it, too, dear."

Mom walked right up to the edge of the shadow but hesitated, afraid to walk in. She turned and looked at us. "So . . . what do we do now?"

"If our *parents* hadn't made us give back the notebook, maybe we could have looked it up," said Tamika sharply.

I stared at the tower. I couldn't see him, but I knew Teddy was inside, along with Bricklayer John, the Krayfishes, and so many other lost souls. Suddenly, I was afraid we'd failed to free them—and ourselves.

"Did we do the whole spell?" I asked Tamika.

"We followed all the instructions," she said. "I said the last words right as the notebook flew out of my hands."

"Did you see any other spells or anything when you were reading the book?"

"Yes, lots, but most of them were simple folk charms the Professor had discovered and didn't really care about. He just wrote them down in case they happened to be useful later. Things to make people fall in love, or fall out of love, or find money—stuff like that."

"He played a trick on us," fumed the Princess. "There must haff been more instructions und now ve vill never find them. Eef I know him, he vill burn that notebook before ve see eet again."

Ashes.

That was weird. The word just appeared in my mind like someone else had put it there. Even weirder, I had heard it in Mal's voice. And as I heard it, I pictured Grandma and Grandpa McShane pouring Dad's ashes into a river in Ireland, even though we hadn't been there when it happened.

I looked at him. "What did you say?"

He shrugged. "I didn't say anything."

"Well, what were you thinking, then?"

"The Princess said the Professor might burn the notebook, so I was picturing it as a pile of ashes, which really stinks. And then, for some reason, I thought about how we never got to see Dad's ashes scattered."

"MAL!" I yelled. "You finally did it—you sent me a telepathic message!"

"No, I didn't," he said stubbornly.

"Yes, you did."

"Prove it, then."

"I can't. But I definitely heard you think *ashes*," I told him. "Tamika, what happened to the things we put in the metal bowl at the hospital?"

She went to her parents' car and opened the back door. "I brought them back with us, just in case we needed them—"

Tamika froze, half in and half out of the car. Then, slowly, she brought out the metal bowl and let us look inside.

The tie, the sock, the hair, the blood—all replaced by a fine layer of ash.

"Burned by a magical flame," she whispered.

"Great, we have a bowl full of ashes," said Mal, sounding like his old, idiotic self.

The Princess had shuffled toward the shadowy tower and was peering into it as if she thought she might see someone she knew. "Eet ees possible that the curse has been lifted, but von more gesture ees needed. Een Rumorian society, great offenses must receive apologies of equal veight."

"The Professor didn't seem sorry for anything," I reminded her. "Krayfish didn't, either."

"Forgiveness, then."

Tamika was racking her brain. "There was a spell . . . a dozen or so pages before the curse-lifting one . . ."

"But who is forgiving whom?" asked Mr. Jackson.

"I'm guessing we need to forgive the Professor's great-grandmother for making the curse and the Professor for wanting to make it permanent," said Mom. "We all could use a little forgiveness for something."

Tamika shrieked—not in pain, but with inspiration. Turning to the Princess, she asked, "Do you know where your father died?"

"My mother said eet vas the northeast corner of the buildink," said the Princess.

That happened to be the southeast corner of the Phantom Tower, right where the towers came together. Together, all seven of us walked to the exact spot where Krayfish had plunged out of the sky and landed on Bricklayer John. It made sense: It was near the place, right by the entrance to the garage, where I'd seen Bricklayer

John standing in the photo. There was a flowerbed there now.

A side door opened, and Dante looked out, wearing his uniform for the evening shift. Seeing us, he nodded slowly and said, "Nothing we planted there has ever grown properly."

Well, most of the flowers were growing just fine, but right in the middle, a brown-leaved bush was barely clinging to life.

Tamika tipped the silver bowl and poured out the ashes under the bush. "I remember this one because it was so simple. Now, everyone join hands around it," she instructed.

Trying not to trample the flowers, I walked into the flowerbed on the other side of the bush and reached out to Mom, who linked hands with Tamika, whose parents and the Princess joined up, leaving me stuck with Mal on the other side.

"Now we're supposed to sing," said Tamika.

"You have got to be kidding me," I said.

"Nope. There weren't specific words, like in the other spells, so maybe it doesn't matter *what* you sing—maybe it's just the singing that's important."

"But what should we sing?" asked Mal.

We all looked at each other. The only song I could think of was "Jingle Bells, Batman Smells," which didn't seem appropriate.

Mom had a faraway look on her face. "Your dad loved singing," she said. "Lots of songs. But there was one in particular . . . I used to think it was so corny."

Clearing her throat, she started to sing.

"Oh, all the money that e'er I spent.
I spent it in good company.
And all the harm that e'er I've done.
Alas, it was to none but me."

Now, I know we were trying to finish lifting a curse and everything, but when your mom starts to sing in public, there's just no way it's not embarrassing. And the people on the sidewalks may not have seen the shadow of the Phantom Tower rising above them, but they definitely noticed a group of people holding hands in a circle around a withered old bush in a flowerbed.

But Mom kept singing, and as she did, I remembered the song. I could see and hear Dad sitting on my bed when I was really little, singing me to sleep.

"And all I've done for want of wit,
to memory now I can't recall.
So fill to me the parting glass.
Good night and joy be with you all."

I didn't sing along exactly, but I started mumbling the words as she sang them. Mal joined in, too, even though people were turning their heads on the sidewalk and a couple of people had stopped to watch.

"Oh, all the comrades that e'er I've had
Are sorry for my going away.
And all the sweethearts that e'er I've had
Would wish me one more day to stay."

Surprising me, the Princess joined in in a high, warbling voice, along with Mr. Jackson in a rich, deep voice.

"But since it falls unto my lot
That I should rise and you should not,
I'll gently rise and I'll softly call.
Good night and joy be with you all.
Good night and joy be with you all."

The people who had stopped applauded, smiled, and moved on. Maybe they thought we were having a memorial service—which I guess we were.

"That was lovely," said Mrs. Jackson.

"I think the last part was to stomp three times," said Tamika. "I don't know if it matters who does it."

"How about you, Princess?" suggested Mom.

"I am afraid I vill lose my balance eef I step into that flowerbed," said the Princess. "I vill offer that honor to someone from the younger generation."

"We'll all do it," I said.

As we stepped toward the small pile of ashes, I realized I was still holding hands with Mal. Normally, the only time we touched was when we were hitting each other, but for some reason I didn't let go.

I was thinking about how Bricklayer John's grandma's curse had backfired. She intended to curse the family of Vincent Krayfish by imprisoning them at the site of his selfish mistake, and she did—but she also accidentally caught her grandson, the innocent victim of the tragedy.

Of all the people involved, Bricklayer John had handled it best, building a new home for the other trapped souls and patiently waiting until he was finally released.

And even though he never lived in the tower, the Professor—John Junior—had been caught in his own way. As I now knew myself, the real curse wasn't being trapped—it was being unable to let go.

Mal and Tamika stepped forward, and we all raised our feet. When I nodded, we stomped three times, the ashes puffing out from underneath our sneakers.

Someone gasped, and we all looked up.

The shadowy Phantom Tower was buckling and bending. A sudden wind howled and swirled around us while the bricks of the building disintegrated into the beautiful, colorful particles we'd seen released by Bricklayer John's hammer. As the building flickered, they caught the last rays of the dying sun, sparkled, and disappeared.

The wind died as quickly as it came, and once again, honks, shouts, and booming stereos filled the summer night. On Lake Shore Drive, a motorcycle sped past like an angry wasp. I expected to see the people on the sidewalk gaping and pointing, but they moved past like normal, headed out for the evening or home for the day.

I squeezed Mal's hand before I let go, and he gave me a squeeze back. When I realized Mom was watching, I gave him a little punch on the arm just so she'd know we were still okay.

"And that is that," said the Princess.

She had forgotten to use her princess voice, so she sounded like a regular Chicagoan.

Mom noticed, and looked at her funny, but didn't say anything. I guess that wasn't the weirdest thing Mom had seen or heard in the last few hours.

"What will you do now that the curse is lifted?" I asked the Princess.

"Leave, of course!" she said. "Und I'm taking my cats vith me. Before I die, I vant them to see vat's left of Syldavia."

"What will we do?" Tamika asked her parents.

"I suggest we carry on as though none of this happened," said Mrs. Jackson, turning to her husband. "What do you think, dear?"

"I agree," said Mr. Jackson, encircling his wife and daughter in a hug. "Now that the curse has been lifted, we should go right back to living the way we did before: in blissful ignorance."

"And what will we do, Mom?" asked Mal.

"The idea of moving sounds absolutely exhausting," she said. "Unless I get fired on Tuesday, we're not going anywhere."

CHAPTER THIRTEEN

UNKNOWN CALLER

MOM DIDN'T GET FIRED. Instead, the Professor announced his retirement. Eventually, she got used to her supervisor, and her supervisor got used to her, and she started seeming a little less tired and a little more happy after work. She even decided to enroll in classes herself to finish the college degree she'd started a long time ago.

Mal and I started school after Labor Day, and even though he didn't have a single problem with any of the homework, he didn't raise his hand as much as he usually did and didn't go out of his way to let everyone know about the big brain hiding under his neatly combed brown hair.

He had only ever transmitted one word to me telepathically—and it was an important word, too—but I didn't need telepathy to feel like we had a new understanding. I didn't whale on him as much as I used to, and he didn't do anything extra to let our classmates know he was the smart one and I was the not-so-smart one.

Then again, I had solved enough problems in the Phantom Tower that I felt smarter than I used to.

For the next few weeks, Brunhild Tower was busy as trucks rolled up to the loading dock and new families moved in. All of a sudden, everyone had a newfound interest in the historic building. People waited in twos and threes to speak with the building manager. With the curse finally lifted, I wondered if people just wanted to live there again without knowing why.

I, for one, was glad we were staying put. Our best friend, Tamika, lived in the building, after all, and the school down the street wasn't as much like a prison as it looked. And even after all the craziness of the past couple of weeks, nobody wanted to get back in the van for another long drive—least of all Eric.

One Saturday in October, I finally got up my courage and went into the elevator after one o'clock to check on the panel—but the *13* button didn't appear. Just to make sure, I rode up and down for a while, getting some strange looks in the process. But the portal to the Phantom Tower was closed, and I guessed it was gone forever.

I still missed Dad and thought about him a lot, but the Professor's problems letting go of Bricklayer John had helped me realize I didn't have to worry about forgetting him. I stopped winding Dad's watch and eventually put it at the back of my sock drawer. And, gradually, I stopped talking to him at night.

Even then, it was hard to let go of the phone. I knew he wasn't going to call, but I'd had so many "conversations" with him that I had a hard time putting it away. For some reason, I decided to charge it one last time before I did. Once I plugged it in, it only took about fifteen minutes before it came on.

It was an old flip phone, not a smartphone, so I didn't have to guess a code to unlock it. I just opened it up and looked at the screen. Scrolling through his call history, I could see that almost all of them—including his last one—were to Mom.

While I stared at it, wondering what to do next, it rang.

I was so surprised that I dropped it onto my bed—but right away, I picked it up again and looked at the caller ID.

It read *Unknown Caller*.

Holding my breath, I pressed the green button to take the call.

When I put the phone to my ear, all I could hear was crackling static.

"Hello?" I said.

Static.

Then there were a few beeps and the call was disconnected.

When my heartbeat finally got back to normal, I decided it was just a wrong number, or a telemarketer who hung up when they heard a kid's voice.

Before powering down the phone for good, I noticed

an option for a voice memo. There was a number one next to it. I pressed the button.

At first, I couldn't figure out what I was hearing: It seemed like Dad had recorded some random family conversation. I could hear my voice and Mal's. There was so much static and background noise I could barely make out words, but it sounded like we were all kidding around. Mom was there, and she was in on it, too. The original joke must have been told before the recording started, but I could hear Mal and me saying, "*Dad . . .*" and groaning in unison after he delivered a particularly corny punch line. It was probably the one about dinosaurs and wooden underwear.

The recording went on for about forty-five seconds and then just stopped. I couldn't tell what was supposed to be so funny, but I loved hearing Dad's voice, so I listened to it again and again. I knew I'd play it for Mal later, but right then I wanted it just for myself.

Finally, after probably the twelfth time, I suddenly thought I knew why Dad had used his phone to record a weird random moment. It was just this: Our family was happy, and Dad wanted to remember. And his final gift made me realize I would always remember, too.

ACKNOWLEDGMENTS

FIRST AND FOREMOST, I would like to thank Jennifer Vitkus and her pupils in room 322 during the 2016–17 school year at Walt Disney Magnet School in Chicago: Murtuza Ahmed, Thewfic Anwar, Ajax Bachor, Noah Barbas, Benjamin Borisenko, Miriam Buterman, Nabiha Charolia, Finnegan Dennis, Callum Dickson, Claire Doherty, Taylor Fost, Sage Furgeson, Gabriela Gauna, Cosmo Graff, Mustafa Hasan, Tyson Hayes, Kayla Jackson, Emerson Jeziorski, Brennen Jones, Rachel Kane, Ayse Karatas, Serena Lee, Saulius Matusaitis, Alexander Maya, Azaria Muhammad, Malcolm Ripp, Thom Rushcke, Rochelle Sazon, Tarun Shah, Gavin Sheldon, William Simkins, Hannah Simonson, Charlotte Smith, and Mir Sustar. They read the story chapter by chapter as I was writing it, and their thoughtful feedback and great ideas helped make this book better.

I would also like to thank Josh Getzler for his wise

counsel and for believing in my books that didn't find homes as easily as this one. At G. P. Putnam's Sons Books for Young Readers, this manuscript was shaped by the keen insight of Katherine Perkins and Kate Meltzer, and invaluable assistance on my middle-grade journey has been provided by Jennifer Besser, Sheila Hennessey, Katharine McAnarney, and many others; I am grateful to them all. Copyeditor extraordinaire Wendy Dopkin also deserves special recognition.

James Kennedy gave me good advice on an early outline, and the friendship and support of Javier Ramirez has been truly sustaining. Steve Carey taught me "The Parting Glass" more than two decades ago and remains my first-choice partner for singing in public.

Above all, my writing career would not be possible without the patience of my wife, Marya, and my sons, Felix and Cosmo. I love you with all my heart.

TURN THE PAGE FOR AN EXCERPT OF

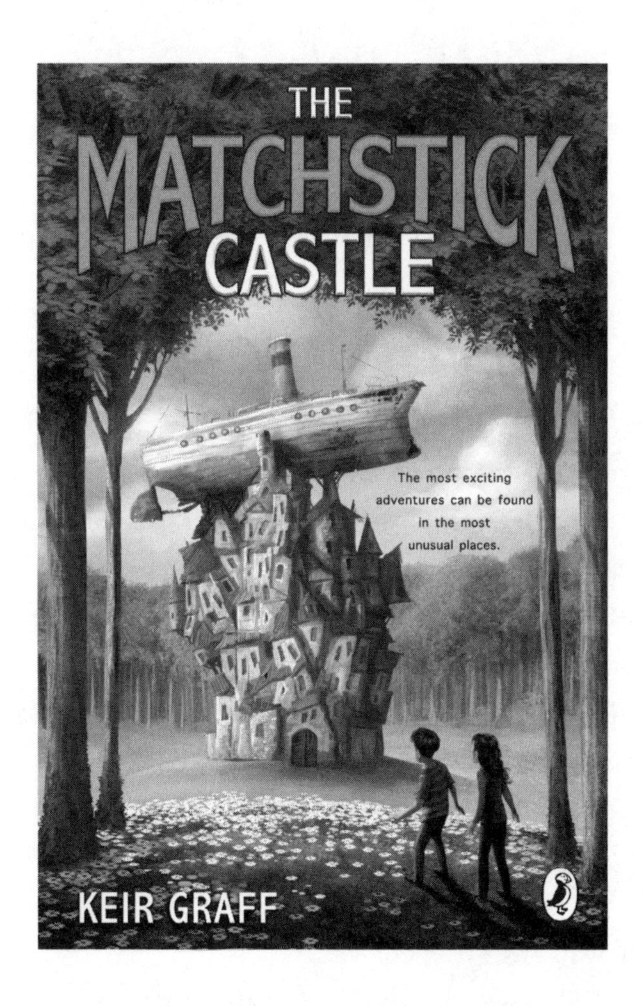

CHAPTER ONE

THE WORST SUMMER EVER

It was supposed to be the perfect summer. I was going to camp out, build forts, have adventures, and score the championship-winning goal in the New England All-Star Under-12 Soccer Tournament. When I wasn't doing those things, I was going to stay up late with my friends, eat as much junk food as I wanted, and pretty much do whatever I felt like until sixth grade started in September. It was going to be epic: the all-time, best summer *ever.*

Instead, I ended up in Boring, Illinois.

No, I'm not kidding. There's a town called Boring. And it is.

How did this happen?

I asked myself that question on the way to the airport in Boston, on the plane, and on the drive to Uncle Gary's house—which was actually just outside Boring, so I guess technically it was *almost* Boring—and was still asking myself that question early on the afternoon I arrived while Uncle Gary showed me how to use the educational software he had developed.

You guessed it: I was having summer school on a computer. Uncle Gary's program was called Summer's Cool, and if you think that's funny, don't laugh. You might be next.

"Now click here to start, Brian," said Uncle Gary, leaning over me and breathing stinky coffee breath into my airspace.

The screen in front of me showed subjects like language arts, math, science, social science, and art listed on a chalkboard in handwriting that was supposed to look like a little kid's. Why do grown-ups think all kids make their *R*s backward? And why would a kid be writing the lesson plan? That's the teacher's job, if you ask me.

Uncle Gary was pointing at *language arts*, so I clicked. A boy and girl scooted onto the screen. They looked like they were drawn by little kids, too—I'm not very good at drawing, but I could have done a better job. I was starting to feel like I was in kindergarten.

"*I'm Darren!*" said the boy, in an annoying little-kid voice.

"*And I'm Dara!*" said the girl, in the same voice, only higher pitched.

"*You picked language arts!*" they said together, sounding twice as annoying. "*Ready . . . get set . . . learn!*"

The chalkboard disappeared, and a story opened like the pages of a book.

"After you read the story, there will be a quiz," said Uncle Gary. "If you get enough answers right, it will let you move on to the next lesson. If you get too many wrong, you'll be prompted to reread the passages that caused you difficulty."

"You really made this?" I asked.

"Well, I did have a little assistance from some *highly* respected educational engineers," said Uncle Gary proudly.

I should have mentioned that my cousin, Nora, was sitting about three feet away on the other side of a folding table in the middle of Uncle Gary's office. She obviously didn't need any help. She had her headphones on and was clicking away like she was getting paid a penny per click. She's one year older than me and about two inches taller. Uncle Gary had spent most of the ride from the airport telling me what an amazing student she was. According to him, she was the smartest girl in her class, the smartest girl in her school, maybe even the smartest girl in the whole country.

And who knows? Maybe he was right. I hadn't seen Nora since I was five years old and I slimed her with a booger at somebody's wedding. I figured she'd just try to get me back—hadn't she ever played booger tag?—but she started crying and I had to go sit in the car.

I'm not exactly a good student. But I'm great at soccer, and climbing, and . . . well, lots of things.

So far, Nora and I weren't hitting it off any better than last time. When Uncle Gary brought me from the airport, she looked at me like I was a birthday present she'd gotten three years in a row. And, in the couple of hours since then, she'd been acting like she wished she could return me to the store.

"Think you've got the hang of it, Brian?" asked Uncle Gary.

Nora stopped clicking and looked up, like she was curious how I would answer. She reminded me of a scientist studying a chimpanzee.

"Sure," I said. It didn't look that hard, even for me.

"Great. Then I pronounce Summer's Cool officially in session!"

While I put on my headphones, Uncle Gary crossed the room, sat down at his desk in the corner, and started working on a computer with two big screens. He was the kind of guy who was hard to describe because there wasn't really anything you remembered about him—he didn't have glasses, or a mustache, or even very much hair on top of his head. If he got kidnapped and the police asked me what he was wearing, I wouldn't have had a clue.

His office was the same way. It reminded me of the big office-supply store I went to with my dad a few months ago when he needed to buy some new report covers for the deep-space data he'd printed out. The store had all these fake offices set up that made me think of grown-ups playing work the way some kids played house. All Uncle Gary's office was missing was the price tags.

The only thing that made it interesting at all was the old-fashioned model ships on top of the bookshelves. I especially liked a fast-looking one with a red smokestack. I wanted a closer look, but they were all out of reach.

Which I'm sure was the point.

If I could, I would have climbed aboard that ship, raised a skull-and-crossbones flag, and steamed right out of Boring, Illinois, forever.

Four days ago, I was walking home from the last day of school, kicking my soccer ball down the sidewalk past the other row houses and making plans for the summer. But when I got home, everything changed in a nanosecond.

My dad was running around the house, trying to do three things at once. While I followed him upstairs to his bedroom, he told me he'd gotten a phone call that morning from the National Science Foundation. If he could be ready by Monday, they said, he could go to the South Pole. He's an astronomer, and one of the most powerful telescopes in the world is at the South Pole. He'd been applying to go for so many years that none of us thought it would actually happen.

As he lugged his suitcase back downstairs, he explained that the astronomer who was posted there slipped on the ice and broke her right hand and her left arm. How do you slip on the ice in Antarctica? Don't they give you spikes or something for your boots? And it's not like you don't know you're on a continent completely covered in ice. But the deal was that my dad would fly down on the plane that would bring the other astronomer back.

"This is a once-in-a-lifetime opportunity," he said, opening his suitcase on the kitchen table and then picking up his phone, which was beeping like it was about to blow up. "I couldn't say no."

My brothers had to be excited, too. Barry, who's cool but goes to college, already had plans to spend the summer in Maine getting certified as a wilderness guide. And Brad—he's annoying but still lives with us because he's in high school—would be peeing his pants because he was going to get to spend his summer working in a pizza parlor and playing video games with his best friend, Isaac. Dad had already talked to Isaac's parents and they'd invited Brad to stay with them.

"Everyone else is getting to do something awesome," I said. "What about me?"

Dad looked up from his phone and gave me a here's-the-bad-news smile.

"You're just as important as everyone else, Brian, but most people already have plans for the summer," he said.

"I could stay with Uncle Sean," I suggested.

If I couldn't stay home, Uncle Sean was definitely my first choice. He was always doing something exciting.

"He's going to be taking photographs in Mongolia," said my dad.

"How about Grammy and Grampop?"

Summer at their house wouldn't be exciting, exactly, but their guest room had a TV, their fridge was stocked with soda, and there was an overgrown, abandoned factory I wanted to explore just down the road.

"They're heading out west to a seniors-only RV roundup. No kids allowed, I'm afraid."

"How about Oscar? Or Diego?"

They were my best friends and my teammates on the Boston Beans, which is the top under-12 soccer team in Eastern Massachusetts.

Dad shook his head. "Oscar's family is taking a Caribbean cruise, and Diego already shares his room with his grandma. But at your age, I'd rather have you stay with family, anyway. I'm sure your mother, if she were here, would agree."

I had no way of knowing what she would or wouldn't have wanted. I never knew my mom—she died when I was really little. My dad talked about her a lot, and there were lots of pictures of her around the house, but he only brought her into an argument when he really wanted to win it. I was doomed.

"Then where?" I asked, slumping into a chair.

"Your uncle Gary and aunt Jenny said they'd host you for the summer."

Of all the places I could have been sentenced to spend the summer—including a desert, jail, the moon, and outer space—my absolute last pick would have been Uncle Gary's house in Boring, Illinois. It's not often a town is so perfectly named for its residents. But Uncle Gary, Aunt Jenny, and Cousin Nora were the most boring people I had ever met. I had never once heard of them doing anything remotely interesting.

"Think of it as an adventure," said my dad, tapping his phone with his thumbs.

"That's easy for you to say. You're *actually* going on an adventure."

Dad put his phone in his suitcase—where I knew he'd forget it—came around behind me, and gave my shoulders a rub. "You never know, Brian. You might have one, too."

If he could see me now, I thought. On the computer in front of me, Darren and Dara were waving their arms like they were trying to get my attention. Their voices came through my headphones: "*We're waiting! Are you ready to start?*"

Uncle Gary looked up. I guess he noticed that Nora was the only one clicking.

"Is there a problem, Brian?" he asked in that tone people use when they already think there is a problem, and the problem is you.

I took off my headphones. "It's just that my dad never said anything about summer school. I wouldn't have to do this if I was at home."

"Studies show that, over long summer vacations, most kids forget a large portion of what they learned during the previous year, Brian. They take two steps forward and one step back."

Uncle Gary spoke slowly, like he wasn't sure I would

understand. He even illustrated the two steps forward and one step back with his hand, like his fingers were little legs walking. I wondered if my dad had told him I was bad at school.

"That's why I created the Summer's Cool software," he continued. "You and Nora are my beta testers. And you're the first ones to benefit."

Nora, of course, had stopped clicking and was watching me again. I swear I still hadn't seen her blink. You'd think her eyeballs would dry out.

"Did my dad say I have to do this?"

"He agreed that you would abide by my rules while living in my house."

"But . . . he didn't say I had to do this *specifically*?"

"These plans all came together very quickly, as you know. We didn't have time to discuss *every* detail."

"I want to ask him. If he never had me do summer school before, I don't know why he would suddenly want me to start doing it now."

Uncle Gary's face tightened, like a smile and a frown were at war beneath the surface.

"Fine," he said. "Ask your father. But until he replies, we'll do things my way. Deal?"

"Okay," I said.

For now, I thought.

Uncle Gary turned back to his own computer.

Nora was still staring at me. I gave her my best what-are-YOU-looking-at face, but she didn't blink. So I tried my zombie face instead: I opened my mouth so far it looked like my jaw was broken and rolled my eyes back until I could practically see my own brain. She stared at me for a few more seconds and then calmly went back to work.

What a freak!

I put the headphones on again.

"*We're waiting!*" chorused the kids on the computer. "*Are you ready to start?*"

I hit pause, and mute, then opened a new browser window and signed on to my e-mail. I knew my dad was still on his way to Antarctica, but I wanted my message to be waiting for him when he got there.

Dear Dad,

So far, this is the worst summer ever. Nora still hates me, and even worse, Uncle Gary is using us as human guinea pigs for this dumb software he made called Summer's Cool. I told him you would say I don't have to do any kind of summer school, so please tell him as soon as you can. And also tell him it's okay for me to stay up late, to have soda with caffeine in it, and to use my spending money on whatever I want. If Grammy and Grampop drive through Illinois, they should pick me up. I would rather hide in the back of their RV all summer then stay here. HELP ME!

Love, Brian

PS I hope Antarctica is cool. Send pictures of penguins.

"It's spelled *t-h-a-n*, Brian," said Uncle Gary.

I jumped, thinking he had sneaked up behind me. But he was still at his desk, eyes glued to his monitor. Was he using spyware to look at my screen?

PPS This is private, Uncle Gary! I typed.

"While you're in the school environment, I have the right to monitor your computer," he answered in his I'm-speaking-slowly-so-you'll-understand voice. "You can always save personal messages for after school."

"Well, thanks for telling me."

"Now you know."

After deleting the last line, I clicked send, waited anxiously while the computer screen seemed to freeze, and then swallowed in relief when I saw that the message had been sent.

"And now it's time to get to work," said Uncle Gary.

I un-paused and un-muted Summer's Cool.

"*Welcome back!*" said Darren and Dara. "*Are you ready to learn?*"